I0630189

The Church and the Pastor

Walking Hand in Hand

The Church and the Pastor

Walking Hand in Hand

S. Tuanlalsiam

2019

The Church and the Pastor: *Walking Hand in Hand* – published by the Rev. Dr. Ashish Amos of the Indian Society for Promoting Christian Knowledge (ISPCK), Post Box 1585, Kashmere Gate, Delhi-110006.

© Author, 2019

All rights reserved. No part of this book may be reproduced or transmitted in any form or by any means, electronic, mechanical, photocopying, recording, or by any information storage and retrieval system, without the prior permission in writing from the publisher.

The views expressed in the book are those of the author and the publisher takes no responsibility for any of the statements.

Online Order: http://ispck.org.in/book.php

Also available on amazon.in

ISBN: 978-93-88945-30-1

Laser typeset by

ISPCK, Post Box 1585, 1654, Madarsa Road, Kashmere Gate, Delhi-110006
• *Tel:* 23866323/22

e-mail: ashish@ispck.org.in • ella@ispck.org.in
website: www.ispck.org.in

Contents

Foreword

I enjoy reading through the manuscript of this book "The Church and the Pastor: Walking hand in hand" written by Pastor S. Tuanlalsiam. This book highlighted the roles and responsibilities of the Church towards their pastors and also a pastor's identity and responsibility towards their congregation. I appreciate the author's effort and insights that is seen through the book. His vision and concern for the pastor and the congregation to walk hand in hand with mutual understanding, love and care is commendable.

For the many who have been a pastor and preparing to become a pastor, this book could be called a Pastor's Handbook. This book shows the way for pastors to be successful and effective in their ministry of shepherding the Church. I strongly believe that for those who are reading it keenly and with a willing heart to learn; this book could give them many new insights for their pastoral ministry.

This book is also a must read for the churches in order to relate better with their pastors. The Church can start to become a strong and productive Church when the congregation understood the importance of the role and ministry of their pastor. This book is a guide for every individual in the Church on how they can be a support to their pastor and effectively play their role in order to walk hand in hand with them.

I pray that this book will be a blessing for every readers and the book will serve its purpose to the fullest in partnering the Church and the pastor to walk side by side with love and care. Hence, fruitfully and efficiently building up God's Kingdom in and through the Church.

Rev. ST. Jamkhanthang,
Coordinator, Ninevi Revival Crusade Ministries

Introduction

This book titled *The Church and the Pastor: Walking hand in hand* is written through my personal experience and with a burden and desire to see the churches and the pastors walking hand in hand with love and honor. It is also an attempt to reveal the other side or human side of the pastor to the church as much is expected from them unrealistically. It also envisioned seeing the church and the pastor to stand united in the broken society and churches today. As much as the church has the responsibility to understand and co-operate with its pastor, a pastor too must understand his role and responsibility towards the church.

When the term Church is used in this book it means the whole body of the redeemed; all those whom the Father has given to Christ, the invisible catholic church (Eph. 5:23, 25, 27, 29; Heb. 12:23). It also denotes the whole body of professing Christians throughout the world (1 Cor. 15:9; Gal. 1:13; Matt. 16:18) as the church of Jesus Christ.[1]

Hence, this book doesn't attempt to articulate the concern regarding a particular church or denomination. Instead the issues faced by the church and the pastor in a general sense. In the same, manner the term Pastor in this book denotes the *literally meaning "shepherd," used in both the OT and NT in a figurative sense for rulers and leaders*[2] of the church in general and not about a particular pastor of a certain denomination.

This book will thus first deal with getting to know a pastor and who they were for the church in the first chapter, and then in the second chapter the writer will highlight the other side of a pastor. In chapter three the writer will give his suggestions and ways to walk hand in hand with a pastor, and in the final chapter this book will also give suggestions for the pastors on how one can improve their pastoral role and responsibilities.

Endnotes

[1] M.G. Easton, "Church," in *Easton's Bible Dictionary* (Oak Harbor: Logos Research Systems, Inc., 1996).

[2] Walter A. Elwell and Barry J. Beitzel, "Pastor," in *Baker Encyclopedia of the Bible* (Grand Rapids: Baker Book House, 1988), 1618.

Chapter One

Know your Pastor

A pastor is understood to be "the feeder, protector, and guide or shepherd of a flock of God's people in New Testament times."[1] But in today's context, pastors are often attributed unbiblical terminologies and given different names. For instance, they are called Sunday's busy men, lazy, or even worse, Christian *Pujaris*.[2] At times, they are even accused of spoiling the church harmony or not knowing how to preach.

I believe it is wrong to loosely associate such unsolicited terminologies with the present day's pastors. Though there are no exceptions that all pastors are good, such terms are disrespectful to the One (God) who is calling the same people to the pastoral service. There is no denying that there are corrupt pastors and Christian leaders. There are even church elders who have blackened the image of Christ and that of the church by engaging in immoral practices and by teaching wrong doctrines. However, using such unbecoming terminologies point to our ignorance of God's anointing.

Being aware of the situations today, I would not defend the wrongdoings of some of the pastors or Christian leaders. However, I would definitely put forward one question to the people who are busy finding new unbiblical terms for their pastors –

When was the last time you prayed for your Pastor, to help him improve in his pastoral responsibilities and in the ministry of the Word? Paul in his letter to the Colossians encouraged the church to pray for the ministers (pastors/preachers) by saying, *"Devote yourselves to prayer, being watchful and thankful. And pray for us, too, that God may open a door for our message, so that we may proclaim the mystery of Christ, for which I am in chains. Pray that I may proclaim it clearly, as I should (Colossians 4:2-4).*

Before judging or finding faults, it is important to focus on our Christian responsibility of praying; pray unceasingly for your pastors and leaders, as they lead the spiritual warfare from the front.

Being brought up in a pastor's family and having had the privilege of being baptized by my own father, I have had the opportunity to observe a pastor's life closely. As a pastor, my father was the feeder, the protector, the guide, and the shepherd of our family and the church. And from experience, I can deduce and understand that even pastors are not perfect, and they do have their human side of life, just like the congregations. They tend to become a soft target when church-related issues arise, and often they go through tremendous pressures which the church members are unaware of.

Growing up under these circumstances, I realized the importance, if not the need, for the church to walk hand in hand with its pastors. In this context, the church members must know who their pastors are, and what they (pastors) were to them (church) according to the teachings of the scriptures.

Hence, in this chapter, I would like to draw upon some biblical understandings in order to shed light on the role of pastors and who they are for the church.

A pastor is God's anointed shepherd for the church

The first thing that one needs to understand is that a pastor is God's anointed servant, entrusted with the responsibility of shepherding the church. The term *pastor* is derived from the Latin word *passere,* meaning "to pasture" or "to feed"; in biblical terminology, it frequently refers to a shepherd caring for a flock and figuratively of a leader caring for the followers.[3]

The Old Testament principles show God as the shepherd of his people (Psalm 23; 78:56). We can also see that God anointed David to be the shepherd of his people – *he chose David his servant and took him from the sheep pens; from tending the sheep he brought him to be the shepherd of his people Jacob, of Israel his inheritance. Psalm 78:70-71.*

In the New Testament we can see that Jesus, after his resurrection, reinstated Peter by asking him three times to feed his sheep and tend his sheep. And later in life, Peter also instructed the leaders of the church to do the same – *Be shepherds of God's flock that is under your care, serving as overseers—not because you must, but because you are willing, as God wants you to be; not greedy for money, but eager to serve - 1 Peter 5:2.*

Jesus is also spoken of as the good shepherd (John 10:14); chief shepherd (1 Peter 5:4); great shepherd (Hebrews 13:20); the one shepherd (John 10:16). *He will feed his flock like a shepherd, he will gather the lambs in his arm, and carry them in his bosom, and will gently lead those that have their young* (Isaiah 40:11), this is a picture drawn from the pastoral life of Yahweh's care over his children. It is the genuine sympathy of a shepherd in real life. The birth of an offspring in a flock often occurs far off on the mountain side, and the shepherd selflessly guards the mother during her helpless moments and picks up the lamb and carries it to the fold.[4] The shepherd will continue to nurture and keep his watchful eyes upon the lamb until they can become independent. Such are the responsibilities taken up by our pastors who are called by God.

To be a pastor is to take up the role of one of the fivefold ministries of the church as mentioned in Ephesians 4:11- It *was he who gave some to be apostles, some to be prophets, some to be evangelists, and some to be pastors and teachers.* So, we can understand that it was Jesus Christ who entrusted the pastors to be the shepherd of the church, and it is he who entrusted the pastors to feed the sheep of his church with the true, pure, and salutary doctrine of the divine Word.

A pastor is a commander in the realm of spiritual warfare

The second thing that one must know about their pastor is that, he is the commander in the realm of spiritual warfare. By spiritual warfare, I mean the constant struggle between the flesh and the spirit, between good and evil, between hope and despair, between faith and unbelief, and between carnality and spirituality in a believer. Spiritual warfare is waged against unseen enemies, principalities, powers, and evil.[5] Jesus too spearheaded the spiritual warfare during his time; he drove out demonic spirits and went through Satan's temptation after forty days of his fast. He also woke up early every morning and prayed to the father before going through the hectic days of ministering to the people who are under the clutches of the devil and controlled by the power of darkness.

Today's pastors are given the same responsibility, not just to tend the sheep, but also to be the commander for the church in fighting against the powers of darkness. It is their duty to safeguard the sheep from the lions and the wolves, through prayers and through whatever means that God has provided them.

Lessons from King David's life

One can draw examples from the life of David to show exactly what a pastor or shepherd should be doing as a leader worthy of commanding the church's spiritual warfare – *But David said to Saul, "Your servant has been keeping his father's sheep. When a lion or a bear came and carried off a sheep from the flock, I went after it, struck it and rescued the sheep from its mouth. When it turned on me, I seized it by its hair, struck it and killed it. your servant has killed both the lion and the bear; this uncircumcised Philistine will be like one of them, because he has defied the armies of the living God.1 Samuel 17:34-36.*

Here, we can see David sharing his story with King Saul as to how he fought off lions and bears to protect the sheep. Taking his testimony as an assurance that David took the challenge of fighting against the giant Goliath on behalf of the people of Israel and offered himself to go ahead of the armies to fight their enemy. Though the king and David's brothers were at first reluctant, King Saul trusted the God who used David to defend his sheep against the wild animals. As a result, David was sent ahead to face the giant Goliath and, thereafter, the Philistines were defeated.

Similarly, church members have to accept the call and appointment their commander (pastor) received from the Lord. Unless and until one learns to acknowledge this fact, it will be difficult to appreciate and honor a pastor's responsibility in terms of being a commander based on the biblical truth.

Lesson from Joshua's life

Looking at the Old Testament, we can see that Joshua was appointed to lead God's people into the promise land; hence he became the new commander in their fight against the enemy. The people and the army didn't grumble against his inexperience nor the authenticity of his call to lead them, rather they promptly accepted him and conferred their trust on him – *Then they answered Joshua, "Whatever you have commanded us we will do, and wherever you send us we will go. Just as we fully obeyed Moses, so we will obey you. Only may the* LORD *your God be with you as he was with Moses…Only be strong and courageous!" Joshua 1:16-18.*

The trust of the people of Israel on their commanding officer Joshua resulted in their unity and in successfully entering the promised land of God by defeating the enemy. The same principle applies even today for the church in the realm of their spiritual warfare. Hence, for the success and growth of the church, the acceptance, trust, and confidence on the pastor (commander) to lead and command the sheep means a lot even today.

A pastor is an epitome of sacrifice and dedication to the church

Peter rightly claimed his commitment to the Lord in Luke 18: 28 by saying, "*We have left all we had to follow you.*" It is important to understand that pastors are the ones who are sacrificing their lives as well as the opportunities they have in life, in order to serve God and his church. Amidst myriad difficulties and challenges, they took the role of being the caretaker, defending the walls for their church members, always dreaming of a Christ-like character for all the members, and walking the extra mile for the wellbeing of God's people.

Jesus said that he is *"the good shepherd. The good shepherd lays down his life for the sheep" John 10:11.* And this is the same example pastors are expected to display in their pastoral ministry, by sacrificing their lives for the church. Though at times, one might not be aware of the commitment of their pastors, they are there for the church, to care, guide, protect, and give their time and life for the congregation.

Growing up in a pastor's home, I could see such qualities highly relevant in the life of my father as well. At times, I felt that my father spent plenty of his time nurturing the church people, visiting them, and praying for them; but that was his call, a responsibility he had taken to tend the sheep and lead them in the right direction.

Though Jesus was mocked, falsely accused, and his identity as the son of God doubted, he didn't give up on his people; rather he laid down his life for them (his sheep). And even after giving up his own life, people still ignored him. The same thing seems to be sometimes repeating and relevant for us today. We tend to find faults with or misunderstand our pastors, who are shepherding us, without realizing what they must have gone through.

In one of my readings, I came across a heart touching writing on the life of pastors,

The pastor teaches, though he must solicit his own classes. He heals, though without pills or knife. He is sometimes a lawyer, often a social worker, something of an editor, a bit of a philosopher and entertainer, a salesman, a decorative piece for public functions, and he is supposed to be a scholar. He visits the sick, marries people, and buries the dead, labors to console those who sorrow and to admonish those who sin, and tries to stay sweet when chided for not doing his duty. He plans programs, appoints committees when he can get them, spends considerable time in keeping people out of each other's hair. Between times he prepares a sermon and preaches it on Sunday to those who don't happen to have any other engagement.

Then on Monday he smiles when some jovial chap roars, "What a job—one day a week!"[6]

Thanks to the pastors who are true to their commitment and who have not given up on their sheep, amidst difficulties and challenges in their ministry. Indeed, a pastor is someone who selflessly sacrifices his life and time for the church.

A pastor administers discipline in the church

Sometimes, I sincerely wonder how much authority is given to a pastor or what kind of authority a pastor should be having over his sheep. Should a pastor be ever humble before the people, should he use the power that was given to him by God, in order to see things working out according to the vision that he has been given for the church? Or, should a pastor be always a silent listener to the church committee and be used as an instrument to implement what the committee wants to do for the church? Should he speak up or will it offend the members of the church, and if so, will it not harm the harmony of the church?

What if a pastor has a valid view but didn't speak up for the sake of maintaining the church harmony, wouldn't he then be offending God? Should he be all the time seeking to please the Committee and never able to do what God wants him to do? Wouldn't it be better if he speaks up and uses his authority as the shepherd of the church, notwithstanding the prospect of inviting the displeasure of some of the committee/church members, doing exactly what God wants him to do?

The list of questions on the issue of the pastor's authority will not end. It is important to keep in mind that not one person could please everyone in the church, and the same goes for a pastor. Most important of all, the authority given to the pastor is from the Lord, and he is answerable to God. The pastor needs to administer order and discipline within the church with reverence for God; the people come after that.

Biblical examples

Apostle Paul wrote in his second letter to the Church at Corinth about his concern for the wellbeing of the church, and before he signed off, he warned them by writing, *"This is why I write these things when I am absent, that when I come I may not have to be harsh in my use of authority - the authority the Lord gave me for building you up, not for tearing you down" (2 Corinthians 13:10).* Here, Paul was reminding the church that the authority he had was not granted by the church, nor was it authorized under the influence of the committee; but it came from the Lord, and he was at liberty to use his authority for the betterment of the church.

In the gospel of Luke, we see about the authority of Jesus which amazed the listeners – *"They were amazed at his teaching, because his message had authority" (Luke 4:32).* This was the authority from above, though at times the Pharisees and scribes felt targeted. Jesus was doing exactly what he was supposed to do. John the Baptists' boldness in preaching, teaching, and rebuking the sins of the people, even those who are in the high post, cost him his life, but he was doing exactly what he was supposed to do.

Even the prophets of the Old Testament spoke boldly without fear; they had the guts to confront the kings and the community, because the authority with which they spoke was from God. And that's the same kind of responsibility and authority bestowed upon our pastors today.

Here, I'm not withdrawing the possibility of some pastors misusing their authority. Instances do occur wherein some pastors use their status and authority for their selfish ambition and agenda. Such pastors tend to over-rule the people, misguiding them in the name of the gospel. But not all pastors are alike and should not be clubbed together. Therefore, my suggestion here is that we should pray for such pastors before passing on our criticism and judgment about them. When we start criticizing them, we are letting Satan stand on a higher pedestal and putting down the name of Christ in front of the non-believing community. The criticism not only harms the person (pastor) but also ruins our Christian image. Let's pray that God will change such pastors; and for the rest, let's leave them in his hand.

We cannot neglect nor suspect or doubt every pastor because of the transgression of a few others. It is important to be realistic and accept that our pastors have been given the authority to administer order and discipline in the church. In fact, Apostle Paul instructed Titus to use the authority that was given to him to discipline the church he was responsible for – *These, then, are the things you should teach. Encourage and rebuke with all authority. Do not let anyone despise you (Titus 2:15).*

At times, it might not be comfortable or easy submitting to our pastor's devotional and sacred guidance, but it is very essential for us to be following him. We must acknowledge and respect the authority that God has bestowed on our pastors, because we all will be accountable to God for our action.

Endnotes

[1] _____, "Pastor," in *Nelson's New Illustrated Bible Dictionary*, edited by Ronald F. Youngblood, eds. (Nashville: Thomas Nelson Publishers, 1995).

[2] Pujari is the term used for the Hindu Priests, who performs the ritual rites on/for different occasions.

[3] D. S. Armentrout, "Pastor," in *Dictionary of Christianity in America*, edited by Daniel G. Reid, eds. (Downers Grove: InterVarsity Press, 1990).

[4] W. R. Harris, "Pastor," in *The International Standard Bible Encyclopedia, Revised,* edited by Geoffrey W. Bromiley (Grand Rapids: Wm. B. Eerdmans, 2002), 679.

[5] _____, *Nelson's New Christian Dictionary: The Authoritative Resource on the Christian World*, edited by George Thomas Kurian (Nashville: Thomas Nelson Pubs., 2001).

[6] _____, *10,000 Sermon Illustrations* (Galaxie Software: Biblical Studies Press, 2002).

Chapter Two

Knowing the Other Side of your Pastor

People often assume that their pastor is perfect, loving, invariably humble, and consistently optimistic in life. However, these assumptions are not always true. Much like the congregation, pastors have feelings too. They also at times desire to have fun and enjoy life and, as such, may not always be able to maintain that serious look, which unfortunately is customarily expected of them especially when they are in the church. Other than the image they are expected to project, they do have another side.

Hence, like any other human being, a pastor cannot always restrain himself. Though at times he is left with no other choice but to suppress his true feelings within himself and is forced not to express them. This is mainly because of the expectation from others due to which he is obligated to outwardly project his loving nature to the rest of the church congregation, even in times of trouble.

Here, I am not trying to impress upon the readers that all pastors live a hypocritical way of life. On the contrary, I am trying to convey my belief that, as human beings, pastors do have another side to their lives. Again, this nature is not necessarily to cover up their wrongdoings or to hide their real selves. It is only that, a pastor has to restrain himself as it is necessitated of him to behave in a specific manner. This nature or behavior is due to the responsibilities that have been given to him by God himself, i.e. to handle the church tasks with the best of his abilities and with true integrity.

Obviously, he cannot act like a husband to the entire church members but does so only to his wife, nor can he speak to the members of the church in the same way he speaks to his children. As I recollect my childhood days, I could understand that the same was true with my father who is a pastor as well as a father. I got to know the other side of him, may be more so than the church people, especially when it comes to family discipline.

I must admit that on several occasions, I did disobey my parents, at times hurting their feelings as well. These have often resulted in me getting disciplined by my father. But when it came to church affairs, my father transformed into a different person. He would then deal with issues lovingly and carefully; he was such a loving and caring pastor in church that no one would believe me on how strict he was at home. Here I am not exaggerating anything. However, much like my father, every pastor also has the other side of him which needs to be seriously considered by each reader.

This chapter will highlight some of the things one needs to know about the other side of every pastor.

He is not a superman, but a human being

The first thing one should know about the other side of every pastor is that he is not a superman but a human being, just like anyone else. He is at times bound to get into depression or exhaustion in life. He would want to work out the church affairs in his personal way and if it did not work out well, then none should be surprised to see him getting discouraged or angry.

Church members may have the tendency to expect a lot from their pastor, at times a lot more than what he can deliver. They may also fail to consider the humanistic nature of their pastor. It is important to keep in mind that your pastor is not wired differently by God, so that he becomes a superman and instantly meet all the needs of the ministry, or fulfill the desires, requirements, and expectations of each church member.

Let us get it straight here that your pastor is not a special combo pack you get in the mall, nor is he specially designed or wired to satisfy the requirement of every person in the church. You need to let him fulfill his responsibilities in the church, naturally. While you may have your expectations of him, you should also remember that he is also a human being just like you and anyone else in the church.

He can make mistakes

Every human can make mistakes, and the same applies to your pastor as well. You cannot or should not expect your pastor to always be able to do the right thing, or whatsoever he does, should be done perfectly. It is important to realize that even a pastor makes mistakes. Hence, we all need to give him the time to overcome them himself. In such situations, we need to understand his weaknesses and support him in whatever way we can. In fact, we need to be by his side and back him up or encourage him not to give up in times of his personal disappointments and failures, either in his life or in ministry.

It is said that 'a real leader will make mistakes.' A man who never makes mistakes, never does anything either. It is rather more beneficial to make hundred mistakes and accomplish something than to make no mistake and accomplish nothing. Mistakes are not sins, but not willing to get up from the mistakes to improve leads to sin. The stories of David, Moses, Peter and others in the Bible tells us that God raises up his servants from their failures to become great leaders for him. Therefore, God allows his servants to be tested, and he himself restores them and strengthens them through their testing times and failures.

It is also important to underline that when we make a mistake, we need to correct ourselves; otherwise we are vulnerable to making more mistakes. Mistakes are bound to happen in one's life but that should not be the end of it all. We should let our mistakes be the steppingstone to success. We should trust God to help us at our point of helplessness and understand that "*Our God is a God who not merely restores but takes up our mistakes and follies into his plan for us and brings good out of them. This is part of the wonder of his gracious sovereignty.*"[1]

In his book entitled "Stay Alive All your Life," Norman said, "*Who doesn't make mistakes! But the greatest error of all is to let any mistake destroy your faith in yourself. The only sensible course is to study and analyze why you made the mistake. Learn all you can from it then forget it and go ahead. Figure out on doing better next time.*"[2] Therefore, we can say that making mistakes is a part of our life, and even our pastors are no exception, rather practically they were the ones who are more acquainted to the mistakes due to the new ideas, innovative programs and ministry activities they were expected to come up with every now and then.

As I was reading different writings and pondering upon the mistakes which are obvious in the lives of every pastor, I came across one thought provoking poem (writing). The writer, an anonymous author, talks about how he feels sorry for the pastors who are often misunderstood by the people as much was expected from them.

The Poem reads like this –

A Thoughtful Layman

I feel sorry for the preacher
In some little towns;
If he's not a shining angel,
All the gossips run him down.

If he stays at home to study,
He should go to see the sick.
If he goes to a convention,
Why, he doesn't work a lick.

If he visits ailing ladies,
He's a gadabout and flirt;
If he dares to go a-fishing,
His good name's forever hurt.

If he's boosting for the young folks,
He's too modern—he's a clown;
He won't preach old-fashioned sermons,
Fit for such as Grandpa Brown.

If he caters to the old folks,
All the young ones stay away;
And they never ask God's blessings
On him when they kneel to pray.

And an unbelieving farmer
Ridicules his soft, white hands,
Hands that welcome weary sinners,
And then teach them God's commands.

Yes, I sympathize with preachers,
For they're human as can be,
And I know they can't be perfect,
For they make mistakes like me.

The writer of this poem made a valid point when he/she said that pastors cannot be perfect, as they can also make mistakes like him/her. I still remember a few years back in one of our Baptist pastors meeting, we had a guest speaker exhorting us with God's Word. While speaking about the challenges in the pastoral ministry, he had used a football match as an illustration of the church, asking each one of us to identify our role as a pastor in that football match. Promptly, some said we are the referee (Umpire), others pointed to the captain of the football team, still some preferred the football coach. The speaker, appreciating us for being optimistic and thinking that we played such an important role in the football match (church), later concluded by saying, these days most of the pastors are like the ball being kick from one corner to another by the players (church).

I am not sure about your take on that guest speaker's illustration. I also do not know how you look at your pastor, and what kind of an idea you have about your pastor. But whatever your thoughts, let us get it straight here that your pastor is not perfect and cannot be perfect because he is only a human being capable of making mistakes just like you and me.

He can lose his temper
Things are not always cool in the church, and pastors are also not always cool, either. Everyone has a different nature and character; some get angry instantaneously, while others are good at controlling their temper. Some pour out their feelings easily, whereas some are good at containing their feelings within

themselves. Some people get emotional very soon, while others are good at holding back their emotions. Some can be easily identified when they are hurt, while some others can remain as if nothing has happened to them.

As everyone has their own personalities, you need to understand that your pastor might be the one who is really struggling to hold back his temper. Though at time he may seem to be in a bad mood, you need to realize that he is very much aware of the consequences of what his anger might cause. So do not worry, just be patient and never forget that your pastor knows his limits and that he will at a certain point of time come to terms with his mind again before things get out of control.

I am also aware that some pastors are sensitive and hot tempered and are capable of easily hurting other's feelings. If you come across such a pastor and are unable to help out, my suggestion is to keep the pastor in your personal "PRAYER". There is no harm in praying for your pastors' temper, it is much better to pray for than to gossip about his behavior or to criticize openly, because by doing so, you are revealing your own immaturity.

Also remember, such behavior (criticism/gossiping) will open the doors to the devil; he/she will not only capture the weaker brother or sister from the church but also worsen the situation in the church. It is said that if you want a better pastor, you can get it by praying for the one you already have. Therefore, it is important that you pray for your pastor and at the same time realize that your pastor is a human being and has the possibility of losing his temper.

It is also very important to ponder over and consider the reasons for which your pastor gets upset. Sometimes, the problem may not necessarily be him; it could have emanated from the congregation or the church committee. You need to understand this well, because every pastor deals with different people and families, and at times could be preoccupied with other programs with other responsibilities hence could be a bit overstrained mentally. He might also at time get frustrated especially when things do not happen the way he planned. At such times, when he could feel that he is not being taken seriously by the people and has been cornered, either by the committee or by some other church members, this could be the possibility for being upset.

Hence, one need not be surprised to notice the pastor getting upset. It will always be better to ask yourself about the things that could possibly make your pastor upset, and if there is something that you can do to solve the situation, you need to take steps and quietly do the needful.

For example, if you know that your pastor is hurt by someone's comment, or someone has not done the job he or she was or is assigned to do; you could quietly approach that person and politely tell him that his comments might have been offensive to the pastor. Hence, by doing this small honorable service, you would be doing a great service to the Lord and to your pastor. In this way, normalcy would be restored.

When God called your pastor, and as Jesus appointed him and set him in the church, He has also anointed him to his service (Ephesians 4:11; John15:16). You only must understand that whenever your pastor gets upset, there could be also a reason. Anger by itself is not a sin, who knows your pastor's temper may be a great help for others to correct themselves or for them to do the right thing.

Lesson from Jesus

If you see the life of Jesus, he did get upset on several occasions. On one occasion he was angry when the disciples tried to send away the mothers and their children (Mark 10:13-16). He was indignant and distressed at the way the disciples were thwarting his loving purposes and giving the impression that he did not have time for ordinary people. Again, on another occasion, he showed his anger when he drove out *"those who were buying and selling there"* in the temple (Mark 11:15-17). God's house of prayer was being made into a den of thieves and God was not being glorified - hence Jesus' angry words and deeds.

So, let's get it straight here that your pastor cannot always be calm, at times he could surprise you with his anger. But do not worry for there must be a reason for this anger, which is where and when you may have a job to do, as was I already mentioned above. Therefore, it is important to never forget to pray for your pastor; because your pastor is a human being, like us, hence can lose his temper.

He does not know or understand all your problems

The other thing that you also need to understand about your pastor is that he definitely does not know or understand all the problems unless you speak to him about them. For example, there are chances that, when you get admitted to a hospital due to sickness for a week or so and your pastor does not visit you, the reason may not necessarily be that he was too busy or indifferent to visit. It could be that he is not aware of your being admitted to the hospital. You may then be tempted to raise questions like "Why? Is he not supposed to keep track of his sheep? How can he say that he is not aware of it"? It is easy to ask questions after questions about your pastor. But in such a situation, you need to realize that unless you or your family or any one from the church had informed him, it is obvious that he will not be aware of your illness. Therefore, you must convey to your pastor of the things you would like to draw his attention upon; only then would he respond to the situation or take necessary steps.

I still remember speaking to one of my family friends over the phone a few months ago; note the confusion and misunderstanding that took place then. During our discussion on several issues, he told me that he was a bit upset with me as I had not wished him and his wife on their wedding anniversary. He also mentioned to me that many others had wished them through their social networking site and also through the phone, but I had not, thus hurting their feelings.

The truth is, I was not even aware of their wedding anniversary date, leave aside congratulating them. This was also because I rarely opened my social networking account. I apologized to him and asked him the date of their wedding anniversary, so that I could make a note of it and not forget the next anniversary. Although I was quite close to this family, it is important to note that I could not have known of the family details, unless I am informed. Had I known of the details well in advance, all the misunderstandings could have been avoided.

I am not trying to rationalize things here, nor am I trying to prove myself right. But to let you know the fact, that is how many people think about their pastors. They sometimes consider their pastor to be all knowing and all aware of their family matters and of their daily lives. But, to even think or expect a pastor to know all the affairs of his church members is next to foolishness. If a person is sick or is going through hard times in life, that person or the family will have to tell their pastor, if that is not the case, then it will be unjust to say that the pastor does not care about his sheep.

Lesson from Hannah and Eli

Looking at the life of Hannah and Eli in 1 Samuel chapter 1, we can draw a very clear example on the shepherd who was not aware of his sheep's troubles until it was made known to him. In the story, we can see that Hannah, her husband Elkanah and the entire family went up to Shiloh every year to worship and give sacrifices to the Lord. But every time they were at the temple, Hannah spent most of her time pouring out her grievances unto the Lord, crying and weeping for a child.

On one such occasion while Hannah was deeply praying at the temple, she was misunderstood to be drunk by Eli the priest. The scripture says – *As she kept on praying to the LORD, Eli observed her mouth. Hannah was praying in her heart, and her lips were moving but her voice was not heard. Eli thought she was drunk and said to her, "How long will you keep on getting drunk? Get rid of your wine" (1Samuel 1:12-14).*

The scene here reveals that Eli was not at all aware of the agony that Hannah was going through, though Hannah was going through hard times in her personal life. This she had not revealed it to Eli, as a result Eli misunderstood her and suggested her to get rid of the wine. I believe that although Eli made a mistake here, he cannot be blamed for it, because he was not aware of Hannah's condition. In fact, if he was right in his judgment on Hannah as a drunk, we could understand that Eli was doing exactly what he was supposed to do. The starting point of the problem that we can understand in this scene is all because Eli was not aware of Hannah's problem, and that happened because Hannah had not told her problem to Eli.

In today's term, we can say that it was because of the lack of communication between the two of them. Like Eli, your pastor might as well misunderstand you sometimes, or you might even at times think that your pastor does not care about your problems or does not understand your feelings. But before you jump to any drastic conclusion or become judgmental towards your pastor, it is important to see to it that you have already made known your difficulties to your pastor. If you had not, and if you were lacking in communicating with him, then I can assure you one thing, that such a misunderstanding is bound to happen. You need to realize that your pastor being a human being himself would not know on his own or have an understanding to all your problems, unless you tell him so.

As you continue to read through the following scene, you will also notice a very interesting conversation which took place between Hannah and Eli – *"Not so, my lord,"* Hannah replied, *"I am a woman who is deeply troubled. I have not been drinking wine or beer; I was pouring out my soul to the LORD. Do not take your servant for a wicked woman; I have been praying here out of my great anguish and grief." Eli answered, "Go in peace, and may the God of Israel grant you what you have asked of him." She said, "May your servant find favor in your eyes." Then she went her way and ate something, and her face was no longer downcast (1 Samuel 1:15-18).*

Here we can notice three significant things happening – a) Hannah conveyed her situation to Eli; b) Eli understood her condition and sent her with God's assured blessing; c) As a result, Hannah's grieving soul was comforted, and she went away satisfied because of the promised blessing.

So, the lesson that we can draw out from this scene is that unless we communicate to our pastor and make known our situation to him, he is not likely to be aware of our situation. But if we do so, then our pastor can pray for God's blessing to be upon us. Subsequently, we can go on in life confidently and be fully satisfied, at the same time we can also see God working in our life as well, as he did so in Hannah's life and blessed her womb.

If Hannah was not willing to communicate her situation to Eli, she might not or never be able to receive God's blessing. If she had not told about her personal anxiety to Eli, then Eli could have never been able to pronounce God's blessings upon her. Thus, for Hannah that was the only key to her receiving God's blessing – And one of the keys for us to receive God's blessings is, first, we should not underestimate our pastor nor should we neglect him but instead open up and share our difficulties, concerns and prayer requests. Then, as he intercedes for us he thereafter can pronounce God's Blessings upon us, as did Eli, upon Hannah.

One more interesting thing that I would like to draw your attention from the life of Hannah is about her humility before God and her respectful nature towards Eli. When Eli confronted her and mistakenly accused her of getting drunk, she did not retaliate at Eli's misjudgment, rather with all her humility and respect for God and Eli the priest, she addressed him as Lord and politely explained her situation.

To this honorable act of Hannah, as I meditate, I said within myself "Bravo! What a message for Christian's today." Do you realize what made me think that way? Ok, for a moment you put yourself in Hannah's place, and consider yourself weeping and praying in some unusual manner because of your personal anxiety and sorrow; then your pastor suddenly comes in the church and starts scolding you and suggests you stop fooling around, or stop acting in a sentimental way. Under the situation, what would be your response to your pastor, or how would you react?

Practically speaking, I believe that you would probably start quarrelling, or start gossiping about your pastor's lack of understanding to your needs and situation. Like many an immature person would do, you too might have simply left the present church and joined some other. You would conclude that your pastor is not a worthy person and not fit to become a pastor in the first place, as he did not understand you or the problems of his congregation. Having misunderstood the pastor, or having concluded that your pastor has no concern for you (when all the while you had not spoken to him about your grievances), you simply leaving the church would be a great harm done not only to yourself but also to the rest of the Christian community around you.

Let us get it straight here, you need to realize that if you do not tell your difficulties to your pastor, it will be foolishness on your part to assume that your pastor will know all your problems and difficulties, all by himself. Hence, it is very important for you to first share all your problems with your pastor and make him/her aware of things that are bothering you. Always consider that your pastor is not a superhuman being – as many might have expected him to be.

He is not a solution-generating machine

The other problem that many pastors often come across is that they are often considered unknowingly or knowingly as a solution-generating machine (If not by everyone in the church, at least certain people in the church). Pastors are always expected to bring out the best solutions in every situations or issues. If they can, they are appreciated by some, and if they cannot, they are criticized by all.

One needs to understand that pastors themselves are struggling daily with their day to day schedules and challenges which they encounter in their family and ministry. They sometimes find it difficult to cope with their life's situations, and often find themselves in a situation that they at times do not know how to deal with it. So, when you go to your pastor with your problems, it is important to bear in mind that he will not always be able to come up with a quick solution for your problems. He needs time to reason out things, and at times might not be able to come up with the kind of solution you might be expecting. In such cases, if you are unhappy with someone's behavior in the church and if you come complaining to your pastor, do not expect instant solutions. Give him time to think and pray about it.

For instance, if you have differences with your fellow church members and you bring it to his notice, do not simply expect your pastor to straight away go and confront the person with whom you are not in good terms. You need to realize that your pastor requires time to think about your complaints and even if they turn out to be true, he has a big sense of responsibility even for the weaker persons in the church. So, his strategy of dealing with difficult situations could be far different from what you want from him. You might want your pastor to straight away sue the person, while your pastor might be deciding on the 'slow and steady wins the rest' strategy. People often try to use their pastor as their problem-solving machine in every situation of their lives. They want to drag him around to be on their side and use him for their selfish motives, and if they cannot get the pastor to be on their side then they tend to get upset and look out for a chance to charge the pastor or embarrass him in public.

Therefore, it is very important to note that you cannot or should not treat your pastor as a 'washing machine.' That is to use him when you need and keep him aside in the corner of your room when you do not require his services. Your pastor being a human himself will not necessarily not have all the solution to your personal and family problems. Before you start back biting your pastor, you need to give the pastor time to think about your situation or condition, maybe he would first like to pray and ask God for wisdom and for his guidance. Remember he is not a man pleaser, but accountable to God first.

Let us get it straight here as well that your pastor, like you, will not have instantaneous solutions to all personal problems and even that of the other church members. You need to be patient and respect his use of wisdom and strategies, especially the way he should deal with issues that comes his way. We all need to bear in mind that he is always not some kind of a machine with a hundred percent output. Nor is your pastor another instant 'coffee dispenser' but rather he has his own personal abilities to judge and has his own limitations to deal with adverse situations.

His family might not set the best example that the church can look up to

Today, it is often said that pastor's children are one of the most indisciplined kids in and outside of the church. I do not know how far it is true, but I do acknowledge that they are the most visible kids around in the church and outside, because of the status of their father. Sometimes, it is possible for a pastor's family to become the easiest and vulnerable target for criticism, due to the high expectations that the church members have from them. One needs to understand that the pastor's family are also human, and they can make mistakes as any other. So, it is possible that they will not necessarily be able to set the best example that the church can look up to.

It is alright to have expectations from your pastor's family, but at the same time it is also important to keep in mind that you need to have a realistic expectation of them. You cannot be expecting your pastor's family to always have a good reputation, or exceptionally good character and standards of living just because they belong to a pastor's family. They do have their own limitations and shortcomings, just like any other family members of the church. At times, they can also be having differences between themselves, or even with some of the other church members.

You need to give them their own space and let them live freely. Just because their father is a pastor in your church, you cannot be expecting all his family members to actively get involved in all the church activities, or you cannot be expecting the kids to always live an exemplary life in and out of the church. It is equally important that you understand your pastor's family and look at them as another family that can also make mistakes just like any other family members of the church.

As I had personally grown up in a pastor's home, with the pastor being my father, I can understand the kind of expectations the church members have from a pastor. Sometimes their expectations go beyond the standard of one's abilities. A pastor's family is always expected to be quiet in the Sunday school, while the other kids have all the liberty to fool around. We are expected to be in the church services while our friends have all the right to miss out in some of the activities of the church.

If my friends had a fight with the other kids in the Sunday school, the problem was solved there and then and the same was forgotten. But if I had a fight with any other kids or had a dispute on some unwarranted issue in the Sunday school, it became the talk of the church. I used to think that this was injustice towards us as we did not get our freedom like the rest of the kids in the church just because we were the pastor's children.

But as I grew up, I gradually understood the high expectations that have been naturally formed as a standard for the pastor and his family, which we had come to accept. But we, as a pastor's children, also found that it was not always easy to meet the unrealistic expectations nor could we neglect them even though the other children did not feel it as a necessity to adopt them – we obediently followed what was expected out of us.

I still remember an incident that I would term it as one of the most embarrassing moments in my life. While I was in my junior class in Sunday's school, there was a grand celebration planned for Children's Day in the church. Our teacher introduced several competitions for us, one of which was a Solo Singing Competition. Since none of my classmates were willing to participate, our teacher proposed my name. To tell you the truth, singing is not my cup of tea; I simply don't have a singer's voice. However, I had to accept the challenge. Why? Being a pastor's son, I am compelled to leave aside all my predicaments and inhibitions. Further, it was taken for granted that we, as pastor's children, cannot afford to say no, that it was expected of us to obey at all costs, whether we are able or not.

Though, I was extremely uncomfortable about the prospect of singing solo, I nevertheless practiced the song daily. Slowly, I started gaining confidence about the participation aspect of the competition, not necessarily about the singing. My confidence lasted till the moment I stood before the crowd in the church. Leave aside singing, that was my first time standing in front of the whole church. As I started the song, I could feel the lyrics which I had thoroughly memorized earlier, fading away. I found it impossible to cross beyond the second line of the song. Although repeatedly given the chance to restart from the beginning, I simply could not cross the second line. Standing up on behalf of the class and then giving such an inadequate performance embarrassed me so much that I do not have the words to express the feeling I had. The outcome of that unrealistic expectation is embarrassment and the losing of all my interests in singing thereafter.

A pastor's family may not be able to set the best example that your church can look up to. What you can do is to stop having unrealistic expectations and start looking at them as a normal family that cannot necessarily meet your varied expectations, just like the other families in the church.

He may not be the most educated person you would like to listen to

There is a tendency of comparing Christian leaders. This is especially true of pastors of local churches as they tend to be the most vulnerable victims to such comparisons. Today, often times, pastors have to meet some unrealistic and impracticable challenges. They are often expected to be the most educated or qualified person to listen to.

As we live in a globalized world, our worldview has changed. We start prioritizing education and qualification in order to decide whom we should be listening to, rather than looking at the person's relationship with the Lord. Here, I am not trying to suggest education is inconsequential. Indeed, education and qualification are important, but they alone do not dictate everything. People tend to look at their pastor's family background, his qualification, and popularity in the Christian circle. They would sometimes compare their pastor with someone having a doctorate degree or someone who is well known and popular in the Christian circles. But they often fail to count on the commitment of their pastor, and the hard work and prayers that has been put in to prepare a sermon.

So, your pastor might not be the most educated person that you would like to listen to, but the messages could be the most living and spiritually energizing words from the Lord. At the end of the day, what matters the most is not the person's degree or popularity, but the living water that flows out from the Lord through the person who is standing in front of you speaking God's Word.

Let's get into practicality clearer perspective below –

He cannot be the new Billy Graham

Many people expect their pastor to always deliver an evangelistic type of messages every Sunday morning, and in every programs of their church. They always hope that every message that comes out of the pulpit will be exciting, motivating, and thought provoking. But this is something I would like to term as unrealistic expectations. You need to understand that your pastor cannot be the new 'Billy Graham.' Your pastor is totally a different person, having a different personality and style of preaching.

At this point, we need to practically think of the difference between a pastor and an evangelist. A pastor needs to be on his knees every day, studying and meditating from the Bible, and finding new thoughts and understanding from the Bible for each

Sunday message. It is not possible for him to repeat what was preached at least for the next few years, because he always has a sharp shooter in the church who would easily point out the small repetition. In fact, I myself being a pastor have experienced the pressure. I keep note of my sermons, so as to not repeat the same sermon in my church. Though I might have the need to speak the same issues and concerns, I do not allow myself to repeat the same sermon by sitting at God's feet in meditation.

Every pastor is given a big responsibility to exhort the people with new illustrations, new thoughts, and new information each Sunday, apart from all the other church gatherings that run during the week and other monthly special events. So, every pastor cannot be expected to be like Billy Graham, or at least one cannot compare him with the contemporary so-called evangelist. I am not trying to pull down the evangelists nor limit their efforts; rather I am highlighting the differences between them and the pastors. Unlike pastors, evangelists need not be prepared for every Sunday sermon, nor for all the church events. They have the liberty of repeating their sermons, as they move around from time to time, meeting different people. Whereas pastors preach to the same crowd most of the time, hence they are required to preach different sermons each time and avoid repeating the same sermon. Keeping this background in mind, a pastor needs to prepare an average of four to five sermons each month. Hence, the total number of sermons the pastors preaches in two months is more than enough for an evangelist to preach at least a year or two before he/she is required to prepare for another sermon.

Each time a pastor preaches, he also needs to think of new illustrations and stories, because most of the time he preaches to the same congregation. Whereas an evangelist preaches to a new crowd each time, because he travels to different places. Hence, he has the liberty to preach the same sermon and repeat it as many times as he wanted to. An evangelist also has the freedom to give the same illustration and story again and again, making his efforts much easier than that of the pastor. Therefore, unlike pastors, evangelists can add a little flavor here and there to make his sermon look fresh each time.

I do not know the kind of expectations people in any given congregation have from their pastors. I also do not know as to when they will understand their pastor's case and stop comparing him to visiting evangelists who come for a visit once or twice a year. I do understand one thing, which is, pastors cannot necessarily be the new 'Billy Graham' of this generation, nor can their sermons always be as attractive as the sermons of the visiting evangelists.

There is a poem entitled, "Preach us a Sermon," which goes very much in the line with the sermons demanded of the pastors or preachers. The poem, by an anonymous writer, clearly reflects the views of many churchgoers of today and their unrealistic expectations.

"Preach Us A Sermon"

Preach us a sermon, Preacher,
But don't preach very long;
Just tell the story of Christ's love,
But don't condemn the wrong.
Say not a thing of doctrines false,
Lest others be offended.
Then they'd turn away from us,
And call us narrow-minded.

Preach us a sermon, Preacher,
But don't preach very plain;

Let others guess at what you mean;
Don't ever call a name;
We'll sing your praises loud and long,
And keep you many a day,
But make it clear, and you will hear,
"Brother, be on your way."

Preach us a sermon, Preacher,
But say nothing of our sins;
Let us keep on like we have done;
And perhaps we'll make amends.
Please let us dance, and gamble, too,
And go to every show.
Make secure and very pure;
We're human, don't you know?

Preach us a sermon, Preacher,
But say nothing of our duty.
Tell us all about God's grace,
And picture heaven's beauty.
Leave out the things that we must do,
We're busy making money;
We haven't time, can't spare the tenth,
Won't be there Sunday, nor give a dime.

Preach us a sermon, Preacher,
When I have time to die.
Tell all the folks about
My home beyond the sky.
Preach us a sermon, Preacher,
Preach me into heaven;
That's my only way to get to stay
Where Christ's reward is given.

--Anonymous

This poem also tells us the kind of expectations the church members have from their pastor, and how they often want their pastor to preach the things that will not point fingers at them. It is true that many people want their pastor to preach to them about things that will make them feel good and comfortable.

But let me tell you that your pastor cannot be the prosperity preacher, unlike some of the evangelists who pull the crowd to themselves. Your pastor is aware that he cannot please every person all the time. He clearly knows that he is a person who is accountable to God, hence needs to speak the truth to correct his sheep in order to lead them towards the right relationship with the Lord. Not that the evangelists are not, as they too are equally accountable to God for all their actions.

Let us get it very straight here that your pastor cannot be another renowned or world-famous evangelist. He is what he is; the unsung hero. One needs to accept him, just the way he is. He may not be like many of the contemporary preachers who come and go, but your pastor will be always there for you. He is not dependent on five or six sermons a year, but on bringing out to you new sermons every Sunday, all of which are possible because of God's grace and his sincere meditation.

So, it will be best to not expect your pastors to burn crackers every Sunday, but rather accept them just the way they are and receive them and the messages that come through them, because the messages obviously come through them was from the Lord.

He may not be like the pastor next door
There seems to be competition among the pastors at times, but many a times such an atmosphere is created by the church members and not the pastors themselves. Remember that your pastor may not necessarily be as talented as the pastor of

another church. He may not be as smart, or even as educated as the pastor next door. But he is the pastor appointed by God to take care and nurture the people of your church. So, learn to be content with the pastor that God has put forth as the shepherd of your church. I believe that if you are the one complaining and comparing your pastor with the pastor next door, you will do the same thing if you are a member of that church that you are talking highly of today. Because the problem is neither with your pastor nor the church, but with the individual person who is not contented or satisfied with what God has given him/her or blessed him/her with.

It is important to keep in mind that everyone has limitations, and no one is as perfect as you would expect them to be. What I want to convey here is that, like the pastor in your church, the other pastor next door is equally not perfect either. My point is that you need to learn to be satisfied with what God has blessed you with and accept your pastor just the way he is.

Your pastor may not be as popular or as famous like the other pastor. He may not have a sense of humor like the other pastors you know. And, according to your assessment, he may not even have the preaching abilities of the pastors that you know or have heard of. But this does not give you the license to criticize, complain, or start comparing you pastor with the rest of the other pastors around. What needs to be clearly understood here is that everyone has their own strengths and limitations. As a good Christian and a member of any specific church, we should not trouble ourselves comparing our pastor to any other pastor in terms of personality or characteristics. We all just need to be thankful to God for the pastor he has given us.

There is a compilation of sayings of the church people, entitled "Your Pastor and Mine," wherein comparisons and complaints were directed against the pastor. The anonymous writer clearly conveys the situations of many churches today –

Your pastor and mine

If he is young, he lacks experience;
if his hair is grey, he is too old; if he has five or six children,
he has too many; if he has none, he is setting a bad example.

If his wife sings in the choir, she is being forward;
if she does not, she is not interested in her husband's work.

If he speaks from notes, he has canned sermons and is dry;
if he is extemporaneous, he is not deep.

If he spends too much time in his study,
he neglects his people; if he is visible, he is a gadabout.

If he is attentive to the poor, he is playing to the grandstand;
if to the wealthy, he is trying to be an aristocrat.

If he suggests improvements for the church, he is a dictator;
if he makes no suggestion, he is a figurehead.

If he uses too many illustrations, he neglects the Bible;
if not enough, he is not clear.

If he condemns wrong, he is cranky;
if he does not, he is a compromiser.

If he preaches the truth, he is offensive;
if not, he is a hypocrite.

If he preaches an hour, he is windy;
if less, he is lazy.

If he fails to please everybody, he is hurting the church;
if he does please everybody, he has no convictions.

If he preaches tithing, he is a money grabber;
if he does not, he is failing to develop his people.

If he receives a large salary, he is mercenary;
if a small salary, it proves he is not worth much.

> If he preaches all the time, the people get tired of hearing
> one man; if he invites guest preachers, he is shirking
> responsibility.
>
> SO WHAT! They say the pastor has an easy time.
>
> -- Anonymous

I don't know how you may digest the above sayings. I am not sure if you are already acquainted with such comparisons and feel that they are no big deal. But I believe they are very much thought-provoking and relevant in today's church context.

Let us get it straight here that your pastor cannot be and will never be like the pastor next door. You need to accept the fact that your pastor has his own limitations and strengths, and you will not really like it if he starts to copycat other pastors. Let him be himself and maintain his originality. He may not have the qualities of the pastor next door, but you must praise God for the qualities in him. You need to realize that if you support your pastor, you will have a healthy and blessed church. But if you criticize your pastor, you only will invite unhealthy atmosphere in the church. So, accept this reality that your pastor is the given shepherd from God for your church, and he is best suited for your church.

He is often burned-out with pressures

Those who say pastoral ministry is easy are not to be believed. If at all they themselves are pastors, then there could be two reasons for their assumption, first, it could be because they are missing out on the actual pastoral assignments. They may be getting more involved in their office administrative works and not doing what all are expected of them, which mainly involves taking care of the 'sheep of their pasture'. Or, secondly, it could be because they are already so burned out with ministry pressures that they are left with no option but to say what they say due to the pressure they are in.

On the other hand, if they are not pastors and assume that pastoral ministry is easy, then there is only one possible reason and that is, they do not really understand what pastoral ministry is all about. They are saying it due to their lack of knowledge about the pastoral ministry. Often, they are the ones who make their pastor's job more difficult, adding more pressures in the personal life, family life, and ministry of their pastor. The fact is that most of the church members are not always aware that their pastor is the person who at times could be overstrained or burned out with pressures.

One writing that I came across under the title *"Just Suppose, Mr. Businessman,"* beautifully illustrates how much pressures the pastors must go through in their ministerial life.

The illustration reads like this –

"Nearly every businessman complains of at least one ulcer. Think how many ulcers the poor businessman would have if he worked under the same circumstances as the average minister?

"Just suppose, Mr. Businessman, that you were the overseer of 100 workers.

"Suppose only about 50 percent of them ever showed up for work at a given time and only 25 percent could be relied upon.

"Suppose that every time a simple flash of lightning appeared in the sky, large numbers of young workers pulled the covers over their heads and failed to report for duty.

"Suppose your workers only worked when they felt like it and yet you must be very sweet and never fire one of them. To get them back to work you must beg them, plead with them, pat them on the back, and use every means under the sun to persuade them without offending them.

"And suppose you were in competition with a notorious rascal, the devil, who had no scruples and is far more, clever than you are and uses such attractive things as fishing rods, guns, soft pillows, televisions and a thousand other things to attract your customers.

"How many ulcers would you have?"

This illustration clearly exemplifies the situation of the pastors, which most of the church people may never bother to understand. It is probably true with your pastor as well. I do not know if you have ever tried to understand your pastor. Or if you have ever tried doing something that would motivate your pastor to move on amidst the challenges that he has to go through in taking care of the families of the church.

Have you knowingly or unknowingly become a stumbling block to your pastor, adding to the pressures he is already in? Has it ever become important for you to look into yourself and see if you have been propagating things for the well-being of your pastor and the church or if you have been doing the opposite? You need to understand that apart from the church-related pressures, your pastor has his own family pressures as well.

If anyone in the church is sick or gone through major problems, your pastor is expected to be present to comfort the family; he is required to stay alert nearly 24 hours of the day to respond to such emergencies. At times, he has to leave his own sick child and go to the family who may have asked for his presence for their birthday party. At times he has to go and pray for the children of the church families before their exams, and he is also asked to wait back for an hour or two so that the parents could share their personal problems with him.

Often the pastor's own children are waiting for him/her to return home and teach them their lessons or just spend time with them. If he leaves early, then the church members may say that their pastor has no time for them. If he leaves and returns home late, his wife may say that he has no time for his own family. Pastors are very much vulnerable to being disappointed and often suffer burnout due to the pressure of their day to day life. Hence, let's get it straight here that your pastor is human too and you need to extend help when he is under immense pressure. Could you be carrying the load with your pastor instead of becoming the load for him?

He is a pastor without a pastor

Your pastor is also a person who has no pastor to go to. If you need someone to be at your side, he is there for you; if you are going through sickness and in distress, then you can call your pastor any time and he would never say no. But when your pastor goes through problems and the load is too heavy for him to carry alone, he has no one else to be there by his side. Don't you think it is unfair for your pastor to be there for everyone but no one else for himself when he may be in need? Everyone in the church has their personal inner desires for human sympathy and understanding. But that does not mean your pastor does not have any inner desires too. He cannot be an exception just because he is a pastor.

Many a time people tend to think they know their pastor very well, but they rarely are aware of the other side of their pastor. Most of the time they are unaware of what is hidden at the back of their pastor's smiling face. People tend to think that their pastor cannot get depressed and expect him to be always positive in life. What they often fail to understand is that their pastor, who is a human being like them, could also get distressed.

You might be thinking that your pastor needs no one because he is very close to God, and God will take care of him. You may be right in a way, but you also need to understand that Jesus himself was very much close to the father while he was on this earth, but alongside of him, he needed a companion in the form of Peter, James, John, and the other disciples. Even when he took his disciples in the garden of Gethsemane, he took Peter, James, and John a little further, so that he could get their physical and emotional support. As Jesus took the human form, he was not an exception just because he was Jesus the Christ. In fact, he broke down under the agony of the pressure of responsibilities that he was undertaking, hence wanted his disciples to support him in his prayer.

If this could happen to Jesus Christ, there is also a greater possibility that a pastor will also need someone to be by his side at the time of carrying out his given responsibilities. If the congregation is not by the side of their pastor, then that pastor too could be disappointed especially when he is burdened to accomplish the given responsibilities. He is bound to buckle under pressure that builds up immensely. So, the question that you should ask yourself is – who is your pastor's pastor? Who is there by his side at the time of his need?

The question one needs to ask is – Am I by the side of my pastor when he needs emotionally support? Have I given him the confidence to get back out of the pressure he is in? Is he being left alone when he most needed support and motivation?

This is what happened to Jesus; he was left to be all alone by his own disciples when he most required their support. There was no one who dared to stand up on his behalf and speak out for him, when it was expected of them. Will you also as an individual of the congregation of the church repeat the same thing against your pastor? Will you not be there when your pastor needs your support to carry out God's given responsibilities? Or will you abandon your pastor when he is falsely being accused of charges that he is not himself responsible for?

Regarding these issues, someone made a commitment to be the pastor's friend at the point of his need and said – *"I have made a resolution which, by God's help, I will not break. I am determined that my pastor shall know that I love him, that he shall not lack the sympathetic understanding which I can give. As a member of my church I shall, in some way, be a shepherd's friend. I cannot but believe that there are many others like me who will day by day, stand at the side of the man who has no pastor."*[3]

I only wish that you will also understand the amount of pressures your pastor has to go through because of the ministry that he has been called into. Like many others, do not consider your pastor as having no disappointments in life. But rather be aware that your pastor also suffers pressure and burnout. Therefore, like you would need him to be on your side and sympathize with you when you are down, there will be time when he too will need you. The church must also understand him and his family and be on their side, physically or spiritually, in times of their difficulty and need. Could you be your pastor's pastor?

Endnotes

[1] J. I. Packer, *Knowing God* (Downers Grove, IL: InterVarsity Press, 1973), 2I9.

[2] Norman Vincent Peale, *Stay Alive All Your Life* (Carmel, NY: Guideposts Associates, Inc., 1957), 138.

[3] Paul Lee Tan, *Encyclopedia of 7700 Illustrations: A Treasury of Illustrations, Anecdotes, Facts and Quotations for Pastors, Teachers and Christian Workers* (Garland TX: Bible Communications, 1996).

Chapter Three

Walk Hand in Hand with your Pastor

To keep up to your pastor and be on his side in order to support him when he is down or when he goes through hard times is not just a responsibility but a necessity and a privilege for the member of the body of Christ. In the previous two chapters, we have discussed who your pastor is, and the other side of him. But knowing your pastor and understanding, is not enough. It is also important to act in line with your understanding. As I have frequently mentioned earlier, your pastor also needs people around who would sympathize and understand his situation.

Therefore, it will be unwise to always expect something out of your pastor without recognizing his human side. You need to learn to go hand in hand with your pastor. It means that you are there when he needs you; that you will be there to encourage and support when he goes through rough patches. Being a member of a church, which is the body of Christ, you are a part of that body and have a role to play, not to break down the body but to build up the body i.e. the church.

You could be the hand, the feet, or whatever, but you cannot forget to respect, love, and pay attention to the head (your pastor) that God has placed within the body (Local church) on this earth. Apostle Paul in his letter to the church at Thessalonica gave a wonderful instruction in this regard – *"Now we ask you, brothers, to respect those who work hard among you, who are over you in the Lord and who admonish you. Hold them in the highest regard in love because of their work..."– 1 Thessolonians 5:12-13.* Now, the intense questions are - How do we do what God wants us to do for our pastor? What do we do if we are to do something for the pastor? When should we do whatever we are required to do? The list will go on until one actually starts doing something.

Through the years, from my time growing up in a pastor's home to the day I became a pastor, God has taught me many things, through my parents and through several experiences. One of the things that I grew up learning is to show respect and pay attention to the pastors' mission and their work, regardless of their age, background or looks. I remember our house used to be always open for everyone, and especially when it was related to mission workers coming over and visiting us, they were then always requested to stay back for a meal. My parents would make it a point that those pastors or mission workers visiting our home do not leave without a meal or snacks. My parent's gesture to our guests was one of the factors that shaped my life. I still remember when I got married a few years later; I wanted to honor the pastor in gratitude who had solemnized our marriage. So, on our wedding night my wife and I opened all the gifts and selected one of the best gifts for our pastor and his family. The next day we went to his house and gave it to him to show our love and gratitude.

So, if you are still wondering how you could possibly start doing something good for your pastor, I would highlight a few steps to help you decide what you could do. You could also add more to the list as per your capabilities and abilities.

Join hands with your pastor

Joining hands with your pastor is one of the best ways to let your pastor understand that you care, and that he is not alone in the journey of fulfilling his responsibilities for the church. At times, the pastor is expected to carry out the ministry of the church on his own, and often left alone to do the job. Even if he comes up with good plans and proposals for the nurturing and growth of the church, the church seems to not respond to them. And at times it seems as though the church members never pay heed to their pastor's instructions. As a result, the pastor may tend to get discouraged and disappointed in the ministerial life. Pastors need someone who would understand them and join hands with them as they prepare and plan out things for the benefit of the church.

I believe that even your pastor would find himself in such a situation; while you might not be aware of his feelings, he might already be feeling lost within the church ministry. You need to understand, support, and join hands with your pastor as he leads the church.

Be open to your pastor – The first thing that you should remember in order to join hands with your pastor is to be open with the pastor. You need to respond to the new ideas and plans for the church. Let him know that you are ready to assist in whatever he does or feels best for the church. You need to realize that there are many people in the church who are comfortable with the repetition of the old things again and again, and they are not willing to change and grasp new ideas.

So, even if your pastor comes up new ideas and has a lot of inputs for the church's growth, which may inevitably involve the younger generation taking active part in the church ministry, the older folks may often be not interested in the new ideas and plans. There are also chances that, at least fifty percent of the church will not pay heed to what the pastor proposes. This is when you will be required to play out your responsibility, showing that you are open to your pastor's new proposed ideas, and that you would be willing to adapt to the changes   to be introduced in the church. As you join hands with your pastor in this regard, it is also important to note that instead of waiting for your pastor to convince others, you can personally meet with people and tell them of what you feel about the pastor's new ideas.

Promoting the change in the church and convincing others to adapt to your pastor's inputs, could be your initial task. In this way, you can provide a great deal of support to the pastor and he in turn would be encouraged because you have actually joined hands with your pastor.

Trust your pastor – Unless you trust someone, it will never be possible to join hands with him in any venture that he takes up. Until and unless you trust your pastor, you will not be able to build a relationship with that person. This is the same thing with church matters and it involves trusting your pastor. Because of this specific reason as well as the lack of faith in one's pastor, many people within the church are not willing to openly accept their pastor's new plans and suggestive inputs.

Trust is something that your pastor deserves to get from you. You need to trust and believe what he decides for the church will be for the betterment of the church. As I have already mentioned in the previous chapter, your pastor might not be the most educated or influential person in the church. He also might not even be like the pastor next door, but as he is placed by God to take care of the church, you need to have confidence in his vision for the church. You need to let him know that his ideas are valued by you and the church. That you are there to abide by him, to join hands with him like a trusted friend, and that you are there to build a rapport with him which is based upon TRUST.

Give your time to your pastor – It will not be a bad idea to give time to your pastor as often as you could. You might be busy at your workplace, and the only time you get to meet with your pastor could only be on a Sunday. But despite your busy schedule throughout the week, you should try to commit yourself, setting aside say about an hour or two, at least once or twice a week, to assist your pastor. I believe this will be a great encouragement for him. At times you can call up your pastor on the phone telling him that you would be available on so and so time and date for church-related work. By offering commitments, you would be instrumental in boosting your pastor's enthusiasm.

But if you do commit some set time to your pastor, then make it a point that whatever it takes you don't fail to show up on your appointed time. Otherwise that can be a big blow for your pastor as he might already be planning something and waiting for you, while keeping some of his pending work aside. Therefore, it is very important that you keep your promise. If for any reason you are compelled to break the promise, keep him informed so that he can reschedule all of his plans.

From time to time, you should go along with your pastor for house visits. And if you find him to be too busy, you could also do the visiting on his behalf. So, in order to join hands with your pastor, it is important that you sacrifice some of your time and make yourself available for your pastor to help and support him in his ministry.

Support your pastor to support, not to backbite

The second thing that you need to keep in mind in order to become an encourager or a motivator to your pastor as you walk hand in hand with him is to completely support him. No doubt we always have a good number of people who are committed to their pastor, but this does not mean that you always chase him to get him to do what you want him to do. This also does not mean that when you walk with your pastor, you walk just behind him to show your respect to him.

It also does not mean that you speak behind his back to point out something that you feel is not right. Instead, what I am suggesting here is that you should support your pastor and become a steppingstone to success, especially when he is going through difficult times in ministry.

As a believer, it is your duty to not gossip behind his back nor speak against him to others or talk badly about him, especially when he is not around. There are several ways to help and support your pastor

Make use of your phone

People sometimes think that to support or to become a motivating factor for their pastor they need to do something big, something different, or something unusual. But the matter of the fact is that it is not a difficult task; you only need to know how to do it?

One of the best ways or the easiest thing to do is to make use of your mobile phone. What you need to do is, just pick up your phone and dial your pastor's number. Especially during weekdays, you can spare a few minutes calling up your pastor to find out if he is doing well. It is possible that your phone call may be a great source of encouragement for your pastor and the family.

Sometimes, you could also call up your pastor and tell him that you are praying for him as he prepares for the Sunday sermon, and that you are also looking forward to listening to God's Word. This act will really boost him up, giving him the needed strength and motivation as he prepares for the Sunday's sermon. In doing so, you are conveying to him that you care for him. He too would feel good that someone from his congregation is concerned about him and is eager to hear God's message through him. This way, you would be the source of support and be instrumental in making him work harder and continue to do his best serving the Lord.

By taking such steps, you are becoming a blessing to your pastor and encouraging him greatly. You could also look forward to God's anointed sermon or message coming out of your pastor. Yes, all this is done by just a single phone call from your end.

At times you can also send encouraging SMS or Bible verses through your phone. The fact of the matter is your pastor rarely gets such SMSs from the church members. If at all he gets them from the members, they are mostly reminders for someone's birthday, anniversary, or prayer request. You can turn the situation the other way around by sending encouraging sayings and biblical verses to your pastor.

I still remember few years back; we had received the news of my mother being bedridden and that her condition was deteriorating. During the same week my brother had met with an accident. All these news was disturbing and hard to handle, especially as we are not with them physically. But that night we were surprised by a friend's SMS, a very encouraging one which I decided to always have it stored in my phone as a reminder. The message reads, "Every struggle in your life have shaped you into the person you are today, be thankful for the hard times; they can only make you stronger–@ Lanu Jamir."

Though we had not been keeping regular touch with this friend, his timely SMS during the time of our anxieties strengthened us and reassured us of God's divine plan, his purposes and of his ways of working in our life. Therefore, I would like to encourage each one of us to make the best use of our phones, as they can be a very important source of blessings and encouragements to your pastor.

Be a peacemaker

Be a peace maker. Peacemaking or peacekeeping is a challenge for us Christians who claim to have the Prince of Peace in our lives. The responsibility of a peacekeeper is not to provoke hatred but to promote peace and see that peace is maintained.

If you are aware of the United Nations' Peacekeeping Force; they focus their services only in the disturbed areas of various nations. They are supposed to go to unknown lands and live during war-ravaged areas. Last year, God opened the door for me to be a part of the team of Baptist pastors that went on the Holy Land tour from Mumbai. One of the things I observed while on this tour was the UN Peacekeeping Force stationed in disturbed areas along the border of Israel and Palestine. Their presence could be felt and going through such unsafe areas was peaceful because of the UN peacekeepers.

These UN personnel often face constant threats in discharging their role of peace ambassadors. They are always required to make sure that their sole mission constitutes peacemaking, and that they accomplish this peace mission at all costs. Their commitment is commendable, and I believe that such peace keepers are what the churches need today.

As Christians, we need to have the same level of commitment and determination in our lives in order to become true peacekeepers and peacemakers. As Christians, we are called the sons of God and the prime quality expected of us is to be peacemakers, as stated in the gospel according to *Matthew 5:9*, *"Blessed are the peacemakers, for they will be called sons of God."*

So, from the above, unless we are peacekeepers or peacemakers, we cannot become the sons (children) of the living God. This quality is required of us especially when we come across people in our church who talk behind their pastors. Our responsibility here would be to try to make them understand the situation and encourage them to refrain from indulging in such habits. If at all we get assimilated within their discussion, it is important to remember that we are there speaking on behalf of the pastor in his absence. You can also offer your help to those talking against your pastor to take them to your pastor and amicably settle the matter. It may not be advisable for you to go to your pastor and spread gossip; doing so will only make you responsible for building walls between your pastor and the people.

Sometimes, what others are saying about your pastor may turn out to be true. And if that is the case, it is your responsibility to go to your pastor in private and sort out the matter. Of course, you will need to do this prayerfully, carefully, and with love. Even after doing that, you cannot be going around telling other people that you told the pastor such and such. For you should know, the next time some misunderstanding happens, everyone will go and try to prove that they have all the right to teach him and even insult him.

Apostle Paul encouraged the Christians in Rome to do the same by writing, *"Let us therefore make every effort to do what leads to peace and to mutual edification." (Rom. 14:19).* Here, I would like to encourage you to make every effort to do what leads to peace and to mutual edification. For that, you must be at the back of your pastor, not with the motive of backbiting but in support. Thereby one becomes a peacemaker within the church, rather than becoming a gossip monger who promotes selfish agenda against others as well as the pastor.

Pray for your pastor and his family

I do not know how often you pray for your pastor and his family. But you need to understand that praying for your pastor is very essential; you should realize that if the church does not pray for him and his family, no one else would come forward and pray for them. It is the responsibility of the church to always uphold their pastor in prayers, especially before they proceed on to walk through the next extremes of 'anti-Christ like' activities of gossiping and murmuring.

Let me not mince words here but bring it out straight to you, gossiping and pointing faults at your pastor, especially without bothering to pray, are truly an anti-Christ activity; nothing less nothing more. Paul urged the church to pray as he preaches to the people. In *Col. 4:4* Paul says, *"Pray that I may proclaim it clearly, as I should."* This verse speaks very clearly to us that the church is supposed to pray hard for their pastor before they could even criticize him or his sermons.

There is a story about Dr. J. Wilbur Chapman who, in his first pastorate in Philadelphia, was visited by a layman who frankly said to him: *"You are not a strong preacher. In the usual order of things, you will fail here, but a little group of laymen have agreed to gather every Sunday morning and pray for you."* Soon, the group that gathered every week to pray grew to one thousand men and, eventually, Dr. J. Wilbur Chapman had a great success in the ministry which brought many people to Jesus Christ. This change was obvious because the church was willing to sincerely pray for their pastor.

I personally believe that almost any pastor would succeed if a group of his congregation would thus back him up, like in the case of Dr. Chapman. I encourage you to pray in the same manner so that God will show his grace to your pastor and give him wisdom, grace, and knowledge. Pray also that he may be guarded from the snares of Satan and is kept pure in thought and holy at heart.

I am not too sure if even a handful of people would be praying for their pastor before coming for the church service. Nor would they be praying for him during the rest of the week. The church people rarely pray for their pastor's family, and if at all they do, they would be praying only when someone is sick in the pastor's family, but hardly for his ministry.

If you want the best out of your pastor, you need to pray harder, because he has his own personal shortcomings hence needs the support of the church members through their prayers. Therefore, I would like to encourage each one to always remember your pastor's family, especially when you are on your knees praying for your own needs.

Giving a special treatment to your pastor and his family from time to time can boost up your pastor

It is true that you have to give special treatment to your pastor and his family from time to time to encourage them and to also remind them that they are loved and respected by you and the church. Here, I don't mean to say that you need to prove to your pastor that you care for him; he is very much aware if you are really caring for him/her and his family, or if you are merely trying to show off. By special treatment I mean, boost them and encourage them. You should not misunderstand me when I say from time to time; I am not suggesting that you need to love and encourage your pastor's family only time to time. Loving and caring your pastor and his family should not be dependent on your mood but should be an ongoing process.

Few ideas to make your pastor's family feel special and cared for are as follows.

Have your pastor and his family over for the evening

Pastors are expected to visit families when someone is sick or during special occasions, such as birthdays and anniversaries. At times, they also do get an official invitation, but not on many occasions that the entire family of the pastor becomes a part of such an occasion. Many a times the family members of the pastor are sidelined and only the pastor is invited to be a part of such occasions. There could be several reasons for it, but one needs to realize that pastors are most comfortable when their family is around as well. At the same time, they can also be encouraged as they get a sense of contentment when they know that people are also giving importance to their family members as well.

Apart from the special functions and gatherings at church members' homes, the pastor will feel loved and cared for if his family is invited for an evening without any specific reasons. It could be just having the pastor and his family to come over at your home for an evening meal. Such gestures of yours will be a great way to support your pastor's family emotionally and to show them your love. They will also enhance the relations between both families; bringing joy and happiness to them.

Take them out for fun and relaxation

Occasionally, if you can show your generosity by including your pastor and his family along with yours for an outing, it would be a wonderful idea to do so. You could surprise them with an invitation to join your family for a time of fun and relaxation. Depending on your budget, you could take them to a place of your choice. However, it should not be just for the sake of taking them out somewhere. Rather, plan well as a family and try to have the most memorable time.

Such gestures could help your pastor find some relaxation time with his family, away from the pressure of ministry. It could also be your way of expressing gratitude and sincere appreciation to your pastor for his ministerial commitments to the church.

By taking your pastor's family out for fun, you are also training your children on how to be kind and caring towards the ministers. I believe that such a big-hearted gesture from you and your family will truly encourage and motivate not only your pastor but also his family, as they all continue to serve God and the church.

To honor or to respect, one does not need special qualifications
Some people within the church congregation may be learned, while some are less so. But what is more important is their honor and commitment to God. The hard truth in the Christian community is that some are jealous of their pastor. Such people often question the performance of their pastor in order to cover up their jealousy and disrespect for God. Some would even ask, "Why should we do that for him; why can't he do it on his own?"

Sometimes, certain people in the church deem the offerings and tithes given for God's service to be their property. Some accuse their pastor of spending their money and enjoying it heedlessly. They often raise issues on the hike of their pastor's salary and are of the notion that their pastor and his family should survive with the bare minimum.

As long as such mentality exists in the church, the church will be stagnant. The people will never learn to appreciate, accept, and acknowledge their pastor's service.

I hope this is not the case with you or with your church. Even if it is, I hope and pray that such a mentality would soon become history. Love God and love your pastor's family to the best of your ability and see to it, as a church, that you give them love and honor. Remember that to honor or to respect, one does not need special qualifications, but need a special heart.

Let the written words speak to your pastor
There is a vast difference between spoken words and written words. Often it is the written word that is considered more trustworthy than the spoken word. If any agreement is to be made on any specific subject, it is not done with just spoken words. Rather it is the written words that make any agreement valid and authentic.

The spoken words have the likelihood of them being twisted and their meaning altered, thus becoming distorted. What is spoken can lose its value with no guarantee; hence all that is spoken could well be forgotten. But if what is spoken is written down, then the written words cannot be easily withheld but instead accepted as genuine, thereby making it more authentic.

Even as we look at ways in which we should be walking along with our pastors, that is, in a more closer manner than before, and as to how we could be a source of encouragement for both the pastor and his family, I believe that through our written words we can make more sense to them, than through our many spoken words.

No doubt, verbal appreciation by way of conveying thanks for their services would be a source of encouragement for any pastor. Such kind and genuine words will surely motivate them to do more and give their best for the church. However, we need to understand the possibility of certain people complaining and laughing behind their pastor; such people are capable of bluffing around and saying good things about their pastor in his presence in order to please him. But such a pretense is nothing but mockery, an act of hypocrisy which has no real intention to appreciate or speak any good about one's pastor.

This is not to suggest that all spoken words constitute an act of pretense, that they are not genuine or of no value. There definitely are genuine people around in different churches who speak genuine words of encouragement to their pastor from their heart. What I am trying to convey is that there is something that you can do a little beyond the spoken words, that is, the written words. This makes all expressions authentic and the spoken words clearer.

How should one do this? There are several ways; one of the most convenient being gifting an appreciation certificate or a memento. However, this option is very official and, hence, can be given only when there are special functions or programs in the church. The other best possible option is to write a note of appreciation and give it to your pastor.

In writing such notes, you don't have to necessarily mention your name. A simple note could be written on a piece of paper, thanking him for being your pastor. Sometimes you could just tell him as to how blessed you are by the messages every Sunday.

Sometimes, it may be best if your identity is not known to your pastor, especially when you are writing short notes of appreciation. When names are not written, the positive aspect is that the pastor will have the whole church in mind. May be you could just put your note of appreciation on his desk and leave it there. When he goes home and finds a note written by someone to thank and appreciate him, not only him but the entire family would be very happy, greatly motivated and encouraged.

We once had a time for fun and games in our devotion group, where one of our group members came up with a challenging activity. As per the instruction, without us mentioning our names, we had to honestly write the strengths and weaknesses of the others in the group on a piece of paper provided to us ; each piece of paper had our names written on them.

After we had all written down our personal comments about the other persons in the group, the papers were then passed around. He called out our names and gave us our papers back. Each of us read out what the others commented about us. By the way, it is not possible to know who wrote what on the papers. One of the comments about me had a positive impact on me. It was about the devotions I used to take up. The person wrote as to how thankful and blessed he or she was by those devotions. That was the most touching part of all the comments I had read about me. It did not matter as to who had written the message. Knowing that someone was blessed by the way I had been handling the devotions, though the method of conveying the appreciative message was simple, had a profound effect on me; I felt motivated and my desire to serve was renewed.

Therefore, a positive comment can be instrumental in motivating your pastor. What I did leading a small devotional group is nothing in comparison to what a pastor does for the church and the families. So, how much more will your pastor be encouraged if you could write a note as well, may be at least once in a month. I strongly believe that your pastor deserves to receive such kind of notes time to time, appreciating the work.

Such notes will be more than enough for your pastor to move from strength to strength and continue to give his best for the church and labor joyfully for the kingdom of God. Therefore, learn to appreciate your pastor and, at the same time, learn to express your gratitude to him/her; always remember that written words which you could have in your hands make more sense than the spoken words which are often forgotten soon after.

Learn to surprise your pastor with unusual gifts

The fifth and final thing that you should remember in order to keep up to your pastor and to walk hand in hand with him is to learn to give an unusual gift to him and the family. By unusual gift, it does not have to be something that is hard to get in the market or for which you have to struggle searching it.

Whenever people think of giving gifts to their pastor, they often come up with clothes or Bibles. Sometimes the gifts may be sets of teacups or some other kitchen utensils that the pastor's family already has. It seems these gifts are sometime given just for the sake of giving something to the pastor.

Instead of giving the same thing that everyone else had already given, you need to think through. There are several unusual gifts that one can think of and give it to their pastor. Following are simple examples that can be considered.

A gift of magazine subscriptions – There are several Christian magazines or other devotional materials which come out monthly or on a quarterly basis. These publications could be of immense value and blessings to your pastor. Many a times a pastor is unable to subscribe to such materials regularly or do not have access to professionally published magazines.

If at all your pastor has access to any publications, they mostly constitute Christian bulletins and mission field reports, which are sent to them free of cost, two or three times a month. Therefore, I would like to encourage you to consider presenting a good magazine subscription as a gift to your pastor and his family.

It is advisable to speak to your pastor before you subscribe anything for him, because there might be a particular Christian magazine or devotional issues that he has been longing to receive for the family but could not afford it. Therefore, it would be better to ask your pastor for his choice of any Christian magazine subscription. You could then gift a magazine subscription of his choice.

For the subscription, there are several options in line that you can choose from, and for most of them you do not have to empty your pocket; rather you can consider this subscription for your pastor as an investment of blessings. I would say that magazines are an unusual gift which is something worth giving to you pastor.

A gift of daily newspaper subscription – There are several schemes coming up every now and then in the mode of newspaper subscription. The cost of most of these subscriptions does not cross a four-digit number. Nor would it be a big headache for you, if you opted to give this kind of gift to your pastor and his family. Some of the good schemes even have a onetime subscription for two to three years, which comes with a minimal cost of an amount that is below a four-digit figure.

Who knows a daily newspaper may become a reminder of your love and appreciation to your pastor daily? Though this should not form as an excuse for you to not visit to your pastor's house time to time, I think it is a good idea to let the newspaper you subscribed for your pastor to reach his house daily on your behalf.

I believe that a newspaper daily at his doorstep because of someone's kind gesture will be very encouraging and motivating for your pastor. The things that matters here is not the cost of the newspaper, but rather your love and concern for your pastor and the family.

A gift of an internet connection or paying bill payment – Most of the church congregation want their pastor to be well informed of the current topics that are relevant to each one and that he/she should be a contemporary preacher. In this context, the gift of internet connection or monthly bill payment for the same could become great blessings for your pastor's ministry. The pastor can make the best use of such a gift to get in touch with the members and also bring out current issues around the world for prayer meetings and his sermons. Often church members want their pastor to bring out some good illustrations that are relevant to their own situation or problem during his sermons. Hence, internet connection or paying bills for your pastors can become a blessing for him/her as well as the church.

I believe that access to the internet facility in today's world is no longer a luxury; rather it is a necessity and a must, specifically when it comes to your pastor collecting all the important topical references. He cannot be or should not be running to the cybercafé every now and then to collect information required to meet the expectations of the church.

Therefore, I would like to encourage you to think about it and if you think you can make the facility available for your pastor, I believe it will be of great help to him in ministering your church and families. It is an unusual yet valuable gift that you can opt to give to your pastor. Even if it is difficult for an individual, the church as a whole should see to it that this basic facility is made available for their pastor.

A gift of vehicle servicing – Though it may seem irrelevant, a gift for your pastor in the form of his vehicle service would be a great reminder to him he is being cared for. It is not a monthly requirement, but a great thing to do to bless your pastor and lighten one small part of his burden. It is unusual but I believe that such gesture towards your pastor will be a great motivation for him. Hence, I would like to encourage you to take up one of the unusual gifting options and do your best for your pastor's family to show them your love and appreciation for their service.

Chapter Four

Bettering your Pastoral Role

In the previous three chapters, we had discussed on getting to know more about pastors and stressed upon the church's responsibilities towards their pastors. In this chapter, we will shift gear and stress on the responsibilities of the pastors, especially focusing on how they can improve their pastoral role during their ministerial pressures, and also see ways to overcome them.

Fulfilling a pastoral role to the level that is expected is a challenge especially due to the call and the kind of responsibilities the pastor has. The pastor is called upon to guide the sheep, to feed them with God's Word, and to protect them like a shepherd protects his sheep, even to the extent of risking his life for the sheep. Today, we live in a busy world where people hardly find the time to partake in church activities. At times, even if the pastor needs to visit them, he/she first needs to take an appointment. In today's post-modern context, the life situations of people have changed so much that a pastor's role and job profile are not the same anymore as compared to the past few decades.

People's demands and expectations from their pastors are at their peak; therefore, it is important for pastors to reconsider the kind of role they are playing today. They cannot be doing the same thing repeatedly. They need to adapt to the changes happening around them and see to it that they come up with new, creative, and better ideas and ways to cope with the new 'computer-age' generation.

Pastors are required to think harder, work harder and become smarter, as they are knowingly or unknowingly competing with the technology that attracts the younger generation. Pastors are expected to be more innovative in their church activities and to see to it that this new generation is attracted to the church. They need to accept the fact that they are today's pastors, not of the 1980s or 1990s, which means their role as a pastor has become more challenging, more demanding, and more complicated. Therefore, it is most essential for pastors to do their best in order to improve their pastoral role so that they can be effective and make more sense to the present generation.

It is also important to understand that many pastors of today are stressed out due to the nature of the demands and challenges they face. Many of them find it difficult to adjust their work with their family responsibilities and think that they are unable to do justice to both their work and family. Therefore, in this chapter, I will highlight the challenges in today's context; what role the pastors have, the kind of expectations people have from their pastors, and how the pastors should strive through their darkest moments. I will also suggest ways to improve their pastoral role.

Pastoral challenges in today's circumstances

The circumstances have changed today for the pastors and their work in the ministry, which may seem very simple, but is very complicated. Although the community that comes to the church is same, and the pastor also ministers at the same place, there seems to be a rise of diverse cultures within the church itself. Often the pastors are unaware of the new cultures of the present-day generation who bring them to the church.

Today, there are people from the same community and church having different sets of cultures depending on their choices in life. One of the most common cultures that attract the younger people is the 'Corporate Culture', wherein the people working in the corporate sector have commonness though they might be from different parts of the world; wherein they have common rules and common lifestyles.

Some other cultures that exist within the society and church include the 'Techno-Culture'. The people who adapt to new technologies are part of the info-culture. In this techno-community, there is no age bar, as everyone wants to get the latest information and is after the media and internet which give them this information. Though they are in India, they get access to information from every corner of the world. There is also a leisure and consumer culture, which is driven by malls and multiplexes. Here, they are a community within the community who love to spend and get entertained.

So, what we can understand from these is that there are diverse cultures that exist within the same church and it is at times difficult for the pastors to reach out to the group of people having different needs and expectations. And due to such situations, there are several challenges coming up in the ministry of the pastor; some of them are as follows –

Guilt and Despair – The first challenge that pastors need to address is people with guilt and despair. In today's world, we have many young people with a sense of guilt and despair, as a result many of them have lost life's worth and its meaning. They are very much present in the church physically and it is important for pastors to give their time to such people in order to give them the assurance that their parents' relationship failure is not their fault, or their love failure is not the end of the world.

Many young people tend to blame themselves easily for things that are not directly related to them, at times they give up all hope and think that they do not deserve to live on. Here, they need to be sympathized with and cared for by the church. The pastor should be available not to pass judgment on the person who is feeling guilty for the little mistakes that he or she had committed, but rather he should be there to give them hope and allow them to bounce back in life.

Loneliness – Though living in crowded cities and attending crowded churches, there are many people who are lonely. They are the ones who feel that no one cares for them and are not interested to understand them and their problems. Pastors should understand that though many of the church members are busy all day working and have no time for other things, some of them may be feeling lost and lonely within their hearts. Pastors should try to understand such persons who may seem to be full of life but empty within. It is important to understand that many people will not be willing to share their problems to their pastor easily; therefore, it is a challenge to pray for such people. To the pastors, let me assure you, the more you rely upon God's leading and wisdom, the more you will be effective ministers of the sheep who are lonely.

Lifestyle stress – The churches today, especially in urban areas, have a huge number of people who are stressed out in life. Stress is one of the most common situations among the working community and among housewives. Today, working schedules are stressful, and with added responsibilities and high expectations at the workplace, at times it is not just stressful but exhaustive.

Many people are shouted at in their offices by their bosses, and are given target to achieve, though at times they want to turn the tables upside down and leave their jobs, they cannot do it since they have a family to look after. Hence, they cling on to their jobs not because they want to but because they have to just for the sake of their family. As a result, they are stressed and get into depression. Therefore, all pastors should be able to understand this situation of their members and try their best not to add on another work load of the church on such people but rather try to counsel them and encourage them to take life easily and seek God's help in their circumstances.

Divorce and the problems of single parenthood – The problem of divorce and single parenthood is no longer a surprise even among the Christians today. Divorce becomes very common in our society today, which at times is alright by certain families. There are many men and women who are without a spouse, however, still are responsible for the upbringing of their small children who are also burdened with guilt and regret. These young men and women also must cope with their emotionally scarred children. Dealing with such a situation is also one of the most hurting experiences, which need healing.

It is a pastor's responsibility to address and bring back hope in such families through the gospel message of hope and reconciliation. No matter what the issue is, pastors should not be silent on the issues of divorce. If at all things get out of their hands and the couple insists on going ahead with their divorce, the pastor here should not ignore the couple or the family, but rather continue to support them in his prayers and extend his pastoral care to the couple and the children.

Biblical Principles on the role of a pastor and the church

As we have said in the first chapter, pastors are appointed and anointed by God with specific purposes and responsibilities, it is also important to understand that even the congregation has a role to play as per the design of God for his church. There are several biblical principles that we can draw out on the role of the pastor and the church but let us focus only four such principles that we can clearly see from the biblical passages.

i) The man who enters by the gate is the shepherd of his sheep. The watchman opens the gate for him, and the sheep listen to his voice. He calls his own sheep by name and leads them out. When he has brought out all his own, he goes on ahead of them, and his sheep follow him because they know his voice John 10:2-4.

This passage is one of Jesus' parable talking about the relationship between the shepherd and the sheep. The same is applicable in today's context with regards to the relationship of pastors and their congregations, as it also reveals the role and responsibilities of both the parties.

a) Pastor's role as seen in John 10:2-4

- **Shepherd** – The pastor is a shepherd for the church.

- **Calls by name** – As the shepherd calls his sheep by name as seen in the passage, pastor's role is to be close with his/her congregation and know them personally.

- **Leads sheep** – As the shepherd leads the sheep, the role of a pastor is to lead the sheep of the church and not to be led by the sheep.

- **Walks ahead** – As the shepherd walks ahead of his/her sheep, it is important for pastors to remember that they are to be in the forefront and setting examples that the congregation should be able to identify and follow.

b) Church's role as seen in John 10:2-4

- **Hear his voice** – As the sheep hears their master's voice, the role of the congregation of the church is also to have a willing ear to listen and hear their pastor's voice.

- **Follow him** – v.4 says that the sheep follow their shepherd's leading, so what we can understand from this is that the role of the congregation is not just to listen to the pastor's voice but to also follow his/her vision and be submissive to his/her leading.

- **Recognize his voice** – It is also the role of the church to recognize their pastor's voice; rather than looking out for some other leader, they should be committed to their pastor.

ii) *Obey your leaders and submit to their authority. They keep watch over you as men who must give an account. Obey them so that their work will be a joy, not a burden, for that would be of no advantage to you. Pray for us. We are sure that we have a clear conscience and desire to live honorably in every way* Hebrews 13:17-18.

a) Pastor's role as seen in Hebrews 13:17-18

- **Having authority** – This text highlights that pastors are to have authority over the congregation and over all church leaders.

- **Watching over** – Pastors are to watch over the church, especially for the spiritual wellbeing of the congregation.

- **Give an account to God** – As pastors have the authority and are watching over the church, they need to remember that they are accountable before God.

- **Lives an honorable life** – As seen in v.18, pastors are supposed to live an honorable life having clear conscience and desire. They should set an example for the church.

b) Church's role as seen in Hebrews 13:17-18

- **Obedience** – Churches are expected to obey their leaders, especially their pastors.

- **Submit** – The church needs to submit under the authority that is given to their pastor by God.

- **Cause joy and not burden** – The role of the church is to cause joy in the work of their pastor and not to become a burden for him.

- **Pray** – This is one of the most important roles the church needs to play. It needs to pray for the pastor, his family, and his ministry.

iii) Now we ask you, brothers, to respect those who work hard among you, who are over you in the Lord and who admonish you. Hold them in the highest regard in love because of their work. Live in peace with each other **1 Thessalonians** *5*:12-13.

a) Pastor's role as seen in 1 Thessalonians 5:12-13

- **Hard working** – Pastor's role as seen in this text reveals that he should be a hard-working person as he serves God and his church.

- **Over the congregation** – Pastors are over the congregation in the Lord.

- **Admonishing the church** – Their role as pastors is to admonish the church and lead the people in doing the right thing that pleases the Lord.

b) The role of the church as seen in 1Thessalonians5:12-13

- **Giving respect** – v. 12 says that the church is supposed to give respect to the ones who work hard among them and are over them (pastors).

- **Hold them in highest regards** – The congregation is not to look down upon its pastor, rather think highly of him as to the Lord.

- **Love them** – To love and care for one's pastor is no doubt one of the most important jobs for the church.

- **Maintain peace** – Churches are to maintain peace with each other, and especially be at peace with their pastors.

iv) Be shepherds of God's flock that is under your care, serving as overseers—not because you must, but because you are willing, as God wants you to be; not greedy for money, but eager to serve; not lording it over those entrusted to you, but being examples to the flock 1 Peter 5:2-3.

a) The role of a pastor as seen in 1 Pet. 5:2-3

- **Shepherding God's flock** – Pastoral role is to tend God's people i.e. to nurture, guard, and guide the people for whose wellbeing they are given the responsibility.

- **Overseeing** – Pastors are to serve as overseers, by supervising and managing the church or the people.

- **Not by force or for personal gain** – This guideline for a pastor's role also means that, pastors should have self-conviction and true commitment, and they should not do anything for personal gain in order to satisfy their greed.

- **Not oppressing** – Pastors are not to oppress those that are entrusted to them.

- **Being an example** – Pastors should live a life worthy of their status and they should be an example for the congregation.

b) The role of the church as seen in 1 Peter 5:2-3

- **Entrust self to pastor** – As God entrusted the church under their pastor, each member should have the willingness to entrust themselves to their pastor.

- **Ready to follow** – Church members should to be willing and ready to follow their pastor, by trusting him and following the example that he/she sets for them.

A pastor should realize that the church has the right to put certain expectations

As the Lord's anointed servants and being set aside for specific purposes, pastors should carry out their responsibilities to the best of their capabilities. Though they cannot be perfect in achieving everything that the ministry demands, they are supposed to give their best for the Lord in serving the church and looking after the flocks entrusted to them.

In the second chapter, I had mentioned about unrealistic expectations the church may have towards their pastors as they themselves are human beings and not super humans. But that is not to say that the church cannot have any expectation from their pastors. The church has all the right to have certain expectations from their pastors, and these expectations are those which the pastors have to carry out even if the church didn't sound to them as their expectations. A pastor is supposed to have certain relevant qualities, without which he might be assumed to have not done exactly what he is supposed to do, but merely sticking around or beating around the bushes.

Let us see some of the pastoral qualities which the church has a definite right to expect from their pastors.

i) A pastor should come prepared on the pulpit – The responsibility of a pastor is to feed his sheep with a fresh spiritual food whenever he comes up on the pulpit. And the church has all the right to expect their pastor to come fully prepared when on the pulpit. An unprepared pastor may gather up some information and bluff about few things on the pulpit. But he should remember that his congregation can no longer be compared with those of the '80s or of '90s. Today's church members are well educated and clever enough to know if a pastor is bluffing or not. They always have good expectations from their pastors when they come to church to hear him preach.

Pastors are supposed to really work hard and need to realize that just a Saturday night's preparation for the next day's sermon is no longer good enough for the present time congregational needs. They also must understand that there is a possibility that the preaching of a sermon on any given Sunday might have already been heard by some of their church members or have already been read or seen on the internet, which everyone has access to.

Preaching is a ministry to a pastor for which he was first called into; therefore, I would like to encourage every pastor to always come prepared before they step onto the pulpit. If they come unprepared on the pulpit and share a message just for the sake of sharing something, then I personally believe that this is a mockery not only to the purpose of the pulpit but also of their call from God. And in such a case if they hear a complaint from their church members, then such pastors should introspect and be serious about the ministering of the Word.

Having said that the pastors have to be prepared before coming to the pulpit, I would also like to assure them that the congregation will not necessarily expect them to be the best preachers in the world; if it does, then it means it has unrealistic expectations of its pastors. However, the congregation will definitely expect their pastor to work harder and be prepared before he comes onto the pulpit. Here, I strongly believe that as and when the pastor comes fully prepared and preaches, the Lord himself will minister to the people and do the rest. So, I encourage all the pastors to do their best and be confident that their Lord will do the rest.

ii) *A Pastor should be a person of integrity* – Though a pastor cannot be perfect in every way, the church will expect him to be a man of integrity, without a hint of immorality (Ephesians5:3-5), a man whom they can look up to. Every pastor needs to remember that the congregation has all the right to expect him to be above reproach, having no insincerity, but maintaining integrity in all the areas of his personal life and ministry.

The church expects the pastor to be a person of integrity. Church members hope to see their pastor on time; for instance, when he has an appointment with any of the church member's family. They will expect him not to forget the promises, and also be sincere in everything that is done by him. The pastor needs to understand the fact that if the church finds out his ignorance to maintaining integrity in his personal life and ministry; it would be difficult for him to win their trust and confidence back. Therefore, I would like to encourage every pastor to be sincere in everything and try his best to do or follow up on what he may have said, so that he could be known as a person of integrity and be looked up to by the entire church congregation.

iii) A Pastor should have a shepherd's heart – If a pastor is a *shepherd*, then it is obvious to expect him to have the shepherd's heart. As pastors represent the chief shepherd, that is Jesus Christ, it is important that they also have the kind of heart that Jesus had for his sheep. The Scripture tells us that on seeing the multitudes, Jesus' heart was moved with compassion. That is the kind of compassion the church would expect their pastor to display in his dealing with the people in the church.

Jesus as the chief shepherd knows his sheep and the sheep knows him John 10:14. As such, it is also important for pastors to know their church members and letting their church members know them as well. They should have a good relationship with each other, with especially the pastors exhibiting love and compassion towards the members.

They should be compassionate towards the broken hearted and the sick, be patient in dealing with the arrogance of the youth and give counsel to them as well as to their families. The pastors' responsibilities include bringing back those that are scattered, healing the wounded, strengthening the sick, and protecting the healthy, and guide each one into green pastures.

A pastor's heart should be like the heart of a shepherd, who out of love and compassion risks his own life to seek the one that is lost while leaving the ninety-nine that are with him. This is the expectation of the congregation on their pastor, who should love, care, guide, and protect. Hence, pastorship should not be just a position rather it should be a service and commitment.

iv) A pastor should have self-control – The congregation has all the right to expect their pastor to have self-control. A pastor should have the ability to tame his tongue and be able to control his temper. He should not speak in a raised voice at his church members even if someone does wrong, rather he should lovingly make them understand the situation and instruct them and guide them to the right direction. As a human being, a pastor can sometimes be angry. Still, he needs to understand that the congregation longs for love and sympathy. Hence, it is very important for a pastor to be able to control himself. In fact, one of the fruit of the Spirit is Self-Control. Therefore, a pastor needs to see to it that he puts into practice the teachings of the Scripture.

v) A pastor should have a clear vision for his church – As he is placed in the church to lead, the pastor needs to understand that the church members would expect him to have a clear vision for them. They expect to know as to where they are being taken by him, or what his plans are for the church and as to how the church would be after 5 or 10 years. Every pastor needs to have proper plans and objectives for the church. Hence, he cannot be simply doing things according to his own whims and fancies.

It would be imprudent to take everything in one stride yet achieving nothing constructive or meaningful. A pastor needs to take one step at a time. He could set targets, constituting both short-term or long-term plans for the church, and give his best towards achieving them. He should ensure that in everything that he does, he does not fail the church and God.

The most important aspect the church requires to be assured of is for it to understand that the pastor is leading the church with a purpose and a clear vision for the future. The scripture said, "*Where there is no vision, the people perish*". *Proverbs 29:18.*

Therefore, it is important that every pastor has a clear vision for the church and accordingly leads the people, so that the church can prosper and achieve what God wants.

vi) A Pastor should be a Lifelong Learner – I still remember my previous seminary wherein two guest lecturers had come to teach us on Pastoral Care and Counseling. In one of the classes, they spoke about how every Christian leader, especially the pastor, should remain a student and consider being a 'Lifelong Learner'. Even though they had a doctorate degree themselves, they told us that their learning had no end if they lived. How true it is, as a minister one must continue learning and remain a student of the Scripture.

A pastor cannot neglect his studies and expect to keep things fresh and interesting. He must use whatever sources of learning available, continuing to remain a Bible student all his life. Just because he may have a vast experience in his ministry he cannot ignore his studies. As a pastor, he must see as to how he could apply himself effectively to meet the needs of his congregation. And to do that, he needs to be a 'Lifelong Learner'. He also has to realize that the church as a whole has the right to expect him to remain a student of God's Word all his life by becoming a 'Lifelong Learner'.

Striving through your darkest night

Life is not always easy; everyone has a time of struggles and trials in their lives. Every struggle and hardship one goes through is not always the same as it differs from person to person. At times life seems to be unfair and at other times it seems to give a ray of hope. Life fluctuates, it surprises us with the unexpected, and often one wonders what it means to be here on earth, and as to why there is so much of chaos.

This is also true or applicable to all pastors as they too are vulnerable to trials and hardships in their ministry and in facing all other challenges that they encounter. Many times, pastors do get depressed during their ministerial walk in life, although they are expected to be always full of life and remain cool with every situation that they come across in life.

Therefore, it is important for pastors to face the reality in their ministries. When things do not turn out as expected or when they feel they are unable to achieve their set goals, they need to know that it is not the end. Pastors also need to put their faith in God, that he will lead them out of their darkest of nights, because God will never allow them, or even us for that matter, to be tested beyond the strength that we all can bear.

A survey conducted by 'Leadership' magazine on what pastors think about work, home, and lifestyles, as quoted by H. B. London, Jr. in his book *Pastors at Risk*,[1] reveals the following information about pastors –

- 94 percent feel pressured to have an ideal family;

- The top four problems in clergy marriages are: 81 percent, insufficient time; 71 percent, use of money; 70 percent, income level; 64 percent, communication difficulties, 63 percent, congregational expectations; and 57 percent, differences over leisure;

- 24 percent have received or are receiving marital counseling;

- 33 percent of pastors are dissatisfied with the level of sexual intimacy in their marriages; and pastors report 16 percent of their spouses are dissatisfied, which 69 percent blame on their busy schedule, 54 percent on their spouse's schedule, and 35 percent on frequent night church meetings;

- 22 percent seek supplemental income to make ends meet;

- 28 percent feel current compensation is inadequate;

- 69 percent of the spouses work outside the home to make ends meet;

- 67 percent of the pastors feel positive about their spouses working outside their home;

- 9 percent of clergy have had extramarital affairs;

- 19 percent have had inappropriate sexual contact with another person other than their spouse;

- 55 percent of clergy have no one with whom they can discuss their sexual temptation.

This survey shows that pastors do have many things to worry about, and many of them are under pressure. Though the survey was taken in the western context, I believe that most of them will be relevant if we are to take the same survey here in India.

We have seen in the second chapter that the pastoral ministry is not an easy task; it needs a lot of strength and patience to endure the heat in the ministry and needs a strong determination to move on, no matter what one encounters.

So, dear pastors, as you continue to work in the vineyards of God, I would like to encourage you to stand firm and continue to do the good work you have started, just *"...Be strong and courageous. Do not be terrified; do not be discouraged, for the Lord your God will be with you wherever you go,"* Joshua 1:9, and he will be your guide even during the darkest night of your life. Though there would be thorns on the way, with Satan trying hard to convince you that you cannot move on, telling you that only failure awaits you, just remind yourself of the faithfulness of God that you have experienced in the past, and count on the promises of the cross. The grace of God is far beyond what you could fathom because that is more than enough to carry you through all your darkest of nights.

There was a story told about a pastor who was harassed by members of his church and was very sharply criticized. As a result, he went through depression and wanted to give up his ministry or at least wished he could go to another church. With this in his heart, he went to his bishop telling him that he no longer could endure, and that he would like to resign.

But to his surprise the bishop asked him a few questions instead of having any further conversation on the issue.

He asked him, "Did your people ever spit in your face?"

"No, of course not," the pastor replied.

"Did they ever smite you in your face?"

"No."

"Have they torn your clothes apart and undressed you, or even mocked you?", asked the bishop.

"No," he replied.

"Have they stripped you naked and scourged you or have they put a crown of thorns on your head or have they — crucified you on the cross—?"

The pastor realized and understood what his bishop wanted to convey in response to his complaints.

In response the pastor said, "No, they have not done anything, but may God help me, until they do that, I will hold on."

Indeed, it is true that many pastors tend to get dejected or disappointed during their ministerial walk, but let me reassure every pastor at this stage that the message of the cross is powerful, and as long as they truly understand its message, only then will it become easy for them to carry their own load and find satisfaction in their ministry, even though they may go through moments of undesired experiences.

As we ponder upon this particular point of striving through ones darkest of nights experiences, let me assure each of them of the ten very practical steps that they should keep in mind in order to survive through their ministerial walk, the ten practical steps as penned by Dr. Kevin Riggs, under the title –

Ten Commandments for Ministry Survival[2]

i) Thou shalt not let others steal thy joy. Joy is a fruit of the Spirit and is determined by my relationship with Jesus Christ. Allowing others to steal my joy amounts to saying joy comes from people instead of God

ii) Thou shalt not gripe and complain when people act like people. Jesus saw people as sheep scattered without a shepherd. Which shepherd would scorn his sheep for acting like sheep? When people whine and grumble, they are acting like people— doing what comes naturally. The purpose of ministry is to enable people to do what comes supernaturally. If people acted like Jesus wanted them to act 'I' would be out of a job. (NOTE: I am a "people" and I hope others will forgive me when 'I' act like one.)

iii) Thou shalt keep a positive attitude in all things. My attitude determines my altitude. I cannot control what happens to me, but I can control how I respond. Remaining positive does not mean I ignore reality. It does mean I know God is in control, the church is his church, and he will make sure everything works to the good of those who love him.

iv) Thou shalt work with the willing while praying for the obstinate. Most people follow without complaining. Obstinate people are in the minority but if permitted can take the majority of my time. If a captain waits for everyone to get on board the ship, the ship will never leave dock.

v) Thou shalt not take personal criticisms personally. Honest criticism is not personal and is extremely helpful. Destructive criticism has a personal tone. Taking personal criticisms personally does nothing to help me, nor the person giving the criticism. By not taking it personal I will be able to see more objectively and not allow the seeds of bitterness to grow in my life.

vi) Thou shalt place personal integrity above professional success. My integrity is all I have and if I lose it I have lost everything. At times it is tempting to do things, or not do things, based on how I think it looks to others. It is tempting to compare my ministry with others' ministries, feeling jealousy or pride based on perceived "success."

vii) Thou shalt stay focused on Christ. This one thing will keep me from violating #6. It is Christ I am serving, and it is to him I will give an account. Nothing else matters but his opinion of me.

viii) Thou shalt not allow discouragement to distract thyself from duty. Discouragement is the job-hazard of ministry. There will be days when I do not feel like getting out of bed. There will be times when I do not feel like continuing. It is important that during those times I work even harder, not allowing my momentary weakness to dictate my pastoral duties.

ix) Thou shalt not bring ministry problems home. My wife and family are my most important ministry. The home is to be a safe place, a place to relax, and a place to rejuvenate for the next day. Home is not the place to discuss the difficulties and struggles of ministry. God called me into ministry, not my wife and kids.

x) Thou shalt remember thy self-worth is in thy walk with Christ not in thy work for Christ. Jesus cared for me as a person before he cared for me as a pastor. I am a success, not because of my achievements but because of his accomplishment. If my walk with him is what it should be, I am a success even when I feel like a failure.

There are many circumstances that may seem to be difficult to deal with, especially when it comes to pastoral ministry. There are times when things do not happen according to your plan and desire, and also times when everything seems to be out of your control, and you feel that you are completely helpless. But you need to remember that is not the end of your ministry, as there is a greater hope and assurance of deliverance. You must trust God and cling onto his grace for he is able to carry you through your darkest night.

My father's TOP 10 agendas in his pastoral role

Every pastor needs to have his own agenda and aims and objectives as he ministers to the people. He should not be an aimless pastor but instead set goals to accomplish in his ministry. Especially when it comes to a local church management, he needs to prioritize his aims and be able to identify exactly what he needs to do as per the condition of the church. Even as I was contemplating on bettering the pastoral role by having a proper agenda for the pastoral ministry, I decided to consult my dad who was in the ministry for forty years until his retirement a few years back and having a rich experience in pastoring different churches. I asked him to tell me his TOP 10 agenda during his tenure as a pastor for so many years.

Out of the many aims and objectives, the following are the TOP 10 agenda that my father always had while ministering different churches.

i) Spiritual nurturing with a sound spiritual food as pastoral ministry's top priority. It is true that as a pastor is called to feed his flock, spiritual nurturing of the church members should always be his top priority. At the same time, he should be careful about the kind of food he is feeding to the people. It should be a sound spiritual food to build the people up; one that is not creating a misunderstanding of the truth or misinterpretation of the Scripture.

ii) Pastor must have a healthy relationship with the church committee and build a healthy relationship between the congregation and the committee. Unless a pastor can maintain a healthy relationship with his committee members, it is unlikely that he would have a prosperous ministry. He should know every committee members personally and should be close to each of them by building a healthy relationship based on trust. At the same time, a pastor should see to it that the congregation also have a healthy relationship with the committee. He should be the connecting link between them, and if any issues arise, the pastor should speak up and play the role of an ambassador of peace. If the pastor wants to have a growing church as well as a healthy church, then he should focus on maintaining a healthy relationship with the committee and the church.

iii) Whenever a pastor takes a decision on any issue, he should do it with the consent of the committee. It is important for pastors to not to act as dictators in the church. They should not assume that they can do whatever they want to. The committee represents the congregation; hence, the pastors should always take decisions with the knowledge of the church committee.

I personally remember meeting Rev. S. Vungminthang Ngaihte, the then Director of Missions of the Evangelical Baptist Convention in Manipur. I met him in his office in the year 2006, just before I joined the Maharashtra Baptist Society on a pastoral ministry in Mumbai. Through our conversation one of his advised which I cannot forget, was to always take a decision with the consent of the church committee. The reason he told me was that, if there was any complain or objection from someone from the congregation, then I would be able to tell them that the decision was taken cooperatively by the committee. In which case, it will be easier to explain the situation; otherwise I will be questioned not only by that group of people but also by the committee. I think it was a helpful advice and in today's situation it works well especially in administering the church affairs.

iv) Pastor should know the church doctrine and beliefs and must teach the church members. It is important for a pastor to know the doctrine and beliefs of the church; otherwise he can land in serious trouble when a member comes to him for any sort of problem or help. The pastor should know why and what he believes, why he teaches what he teaches and should not be afraid to talk about doctrinal issues and biblical truths. He should let the people know the beliefs of the church and then teach them sound doctrines.

v) Pastor should give equal treatment to all the church members. A pastor should give equal treatment to all the church members. It is obvious that there will be differences in the church; some would be rich and some would be poor, some people will be highly educated whereas there will be someone who are struggling to read or write, some would be talkative while some others would prefer maintaining silence, always remaining calm. But in all these situations, the pastor should maintain equality and there should be no favoritism in the church.

vi) Pastor should not indulge in unwholesome talk and coarse joking with the church members. While trying to get close to the people and to build relationship with them, there is always the danger of doing something in an extreme manner by indulging in an unwholesome talk or in coarse joking. There is no harm in having some fun and laughs with the church members. However, a pastor should keep in mind the possibility of losing one's self-respect and image in the process. Hence, the pastor needs to be aware of his limits; otherwise his behavior may distance him from others who themselves are not comfortable with such jokes and such unwholesome talks. The pastor needs to be on guard and maintain a well disciplined and respectful character and mannerism while associating with his congregation.

vii) Pastor should be transparent and lead a life of integrity. This is one of the most important things a pastor needs to remember as he ministers to the church. The pastor needs to be transparent especially in financial and church administrative issues. There should not be a slightest hint of corruption or immorality when it comes to money and administrating church matters. He should be clean and not have a double mind in dealing with the problematic issues of the opposite sex. Integrity and honesty should always be his policy in dealing with members of his congregation.

viii) Pastor should visit church families and try to understand their difficulties and family situations. Though it is impossible to know all the family members completely, it should always be in the pastor's agenda to visit every family regularly and get to know each one of them and understand their personal situations and problems. Even if he is unable to visit each and every member of his church due to a large membership base, he should appoint lay leaders who would visit the respective families of the church on his behalf, to know and to understand the church families. This will immensely help the pastor in carrying out his ministry besides aiding him in administering each of his church members according to their respective needs.

ix) Pastor should maintain a healthy and exemplary family life Many people will look at the pastor's family life before they listen to him. As such, it is important for a pastor to maintain a healthy relationship with his spouse and family members. A wrong family image could play a spoilsport in the ministry of the pastor; it could even lead others into distancing themselves from him and his family. Hence, he has to maintain a strict family discipline even at the church.

At times, there is a possibility that the pastor's spouse being more of a talkative person than the pastor himself, does all the talking before he could with other members of the church, or she may even seem to overrule the pastor in all respects in the church. In this regard, he needs to confront his spouse personally at home and make her understand what she should or should not be speaking or doing when she is in the church.

One thing is for sure that the pastor will not necessarily be able to have the best family that many could look up to, but he could have a healthy and an exemplary family life by maintaining a good family relationship.

x) Pastor should find out the talents of his church members and make use of them accordingly. It is the responsibility of the pastor to discover the talents and gifts of his church members and encourage them to use the same in the church. As he encourages them to use their talents, he should also back them up. The pastor should understand that he cannot always have a 'one man show' in the church; hence he should include these talents in the church activities and see to it that their focus is on team work. The pastor should not think that it is all about him and the church, but rather it is all about us and our church. He should involve each person in the church, making use of them for the extension of God's kingdom.

In conclusion, let me make it very clear that there are many more ways a pastor of any church could not only improve his ministerial skills but also look into ways and means of advancing his pastoral ministry by improvising his personal proficiency and also by enhancing his individual talent and personal attitude.

Having achieved this, he then could help bring the church to a much higher level by adopting new and modern ways and techniques. This higher advancement to be achieved not only refers to the physical realm but the spiritual as well. Hence, the ways of functioning have to be changed or altered from where they are at present to the place they should be in the future. This is also specially to suit the present context of a local church. It is also very important to understand that the call of a pastor is from God to build the church - His people and his kingdom, and for this the pastor must fully and completely depend on God's guidance.

It is obvious that the task for which the pastor is called into is not easy, and it becomes a lot more challenging if he cannot adapt to new circumstances. If he is not prepared to face the realities in store for him in every ministerial activity, then the road ahead for him becomes much tougher and sloppier.

Therefore, as a final advise, I would like to encourage every pastor to always consider adopting a 'Lifelong Learners' attitude in his life; and to take one step at a time. A pastor must also adopt an attitude of learning from his mistakes and the hardships that come his way, and while doing so, he should never stop trusting the Lord. He should continually walk hand in hand with the Lord God as he works toward enhancing his role as a pastor. If the pastor can achieve this with his God and Savior Jesus Christ, then he could encourage his entire congregation to "Walk hand in hand with him and they would be able to get it straight from him" personally.

"Then we will no longer be infants, tossed back and forth by the waves, and blown here and thereby every wind of teaching and by the cunning and craftiness of men in their deceitful schemes. Instead, speaking the truth in love, we will in all things grow up

into him who is the Head, that is, Christ. From him the whole body, joined and held together by every supporting ligament, grows and builds itself in love, as each part does its work." Ephesians 4:14-16 NIV.

Conclusion

Jesus is the head of the church. Pastors are ordained and anointed by God to lead the church in its spiritual journey. The pastors themselves were part of the church but given specific roles to play in feeding and caring for the sheep of God who are purchase with the precious blood of Jesus Christ. As both the church and the pastor belong together in the body of Christ and under the headship of Jesus Christ they need to walk hand in hand with each other in love and respect. It is disturbing and heart breaking to see disunity and lack of integrity in our churches today.

It is not only the image of the church that was blackened but the image of Jesus Christ. Hence, as seen in this book, it is important for any congregation and the pastor to be able to go in one accord. Both the church and the pastor need to do their part for the body of Christ to grow from strength to strength and to accomplish the mission of sharing God's love to the world. When the body of Christ is not united it is impossible to bear the image of Christ for the church. But to bear the image of Christ and become the light to the world the church and the pastor have to be in good terms and be supportive to one another.

Therefore, I would like to encourage the readers to know one's role and overcome ones ego to see Jesus lifted up and God being glorified in and through the church. We all have our part to play in the building up of body of Christ and if we can all be responsible in each of our responsibilities then I believe that we can be the kind of church build on the foundation of Jesus.

Endnotes

[1] H. B. London, Jr. & Neil B. Wiseman, *Pastors at Risk* (Wheaton: Victor Books, 1993), 34-35.

[2] Robert J. Morgan, *Nelson's Annual Preacher's Sourcebook 2008 Edition* (Nashville: Thomas Nelson, Inc., 2007), 360.

www.ingramcontent.com/pod-product-compliance
Lightning Source LLC
Chambersburg PA
CBHW021449240626
47154CB00005B/1764